Last Tango in Carcassonne

SALLY TOWNSEND

- The -
PARIS
PRESS

First published in 2018
by
The Paris Press

Cover design by The Paris Press based on an
original drawing by Brian Townsend

About the Author

Sally was born and bought up in Warwickshire with her twin brother. She had an early brush with fame when the pair were photographed in a Bendix twin-tub washing-machine for an advert which appeared on large billboards throughout the UK.

Proud mother of two talented children, Sally now lives in Dorset with her husband Julian. Though *Last Tango in Carcassonne* is her debut novel, she began writing a blog during the years when she was based in France.

In her spare time, Sally runs a vintage clothes stall at her local market in Bridport. When the mood takes her, she jumps into a gig and rows around Dorset's beautiful Jurassic coast.

Acknowledgements

With enormous thanks to those who encouraged me to write. My
beloved father – sadly no longer with us – my ever-supportive mother,
my children, Toby and Tallulah, my publisher Lisa Eveleigh, and
friends in Dorset and Carcassonne who contributed so much. Without
their enthusiasm and support I would never have started.

Thanks also to Julian, for listening.

Dedication

To T & T, with all my love.

L'Hôpital Part One

Finding herself in hospital was a tremendous shock to Serena.

But there were compensations. The ungainly and ugly gown felt oddly wanton and luxurious as she basked in the sudden peace. The pressure had all eased; the multi-coloured merry go round with the frighteningly garish and hostile horses hurtling round and round had stopped. The loud music had ceased, and she could calmly dismount.

Tentatively she put her feet down to the utilitarian flooring beneath her. Her gown rode up over her shaky knees and slipped down over her shoulder but the movement barely registered. Her hands seemed small and useless as she clumsily gripped the sides of the metal bed frame lest she should topple forwards. All her anxieties, all her recent nightmares disintegrated. She knew then, as she would feel even more acutely later, that someone who cared very much indeed was watching over her. She gave silent and grateful thanks to the unknown spirit.

The handsome doctors who then swept in were kind but firm and to the point. 'You have had a stroke' they informed her. She assured them that there must be a mistake but deep down where the truth cannot hide and refuses to be silenced, she had to accept their prognosis. She felt as though she had been tossed ashore and discarded after a ferocious storm at sea, days and nights blurring as she battled the perilous waves that threatened to engulf her. In the past, she had tried to save others from the consequences of their own actions, but in the end, she had needed to break away. For she knew they would try to pull into the dark depths and crevices from which there was no escape. There are places where no light will ever penetrate, and she did not intend to go there. She was a survivor and she would not drown and join the unhappy chorus of lost souls.

But gradually, an inexplicable and mysterious transformation was taking place inside her. She would later state that it was the stirring of her soul and that her future life, her happiness combined with fulfilment and contentment were set on yet another course.

Though frightened by her sudden transition from 'well' to 'at risk', her feisty spirit was unquenched. She was adamant that she would NOT, under any circumstances, be persuaded into the hospital's MRI machine.

Serena's consultant was patient, speaking with a kindness and understanding which she felt grateful for, but he remained doggedly insistent that it was a necessary procedure for stroke victims. An *unnecessary* evil, in Serena's opinion. The thought of being enclosed in the body scanner left her gripped by a hideous, inexplicable terror.

Lying on the hard hospital bed in her pristine room, she tried to justify her fear to her worried son Sebastian, speculating that sharing her mother's womb with her twin might have triggered this reaction. 'I think maybe I've always subconsciously fought for space ever since' she explained, forlornly.

'Don't be so bloody ridiculous, Mum' Sebastian retorted.

So that was that, it seemed.

The hospital porter cheerily wheeled in the trolley. 'Off we go' he announced.

'I can't, I'm much too anxious' Serena said, 'I need drugs to calm me down' and added, as if as an afterthought, 'lots of them'.

Her bad-fairy wish was granted. Yet by the time she had reached the side room and viewed the monstrous gleaming machine she felt the hysteria rising within her. She simply couldn't help it, it was as though an alien had entered her body and turned her into a gibbering wreck. 'I'm just not calm enough' she shouted, hearing the panic in her own voice. The medics looked at her with ill-disguised impatience, but when she began to try and climb out of her wheelchair they capitulated and wheeled her back up to her room in disgrace.

Eventually, another doctor appeared and gave her a shot, telling her sternly that there was just this one chance to establish the severity of her condition. After that, it was her personal choice not to be helped.

'We need to ascertain that there is no damage to your brain tissue' he explained. 'There's nothing wrong with my brain' she insisted, but looking at Sebastian's troubled face, she did privately wonder if her behaviour was an indication that she was losing - or had lost - the plot completely. The second shot did nothing to alter her mood. 'I don't know what drugs you use' she muttered sulkily, 'but they're crap'.

A placid elderly gentleman lay contentedly on the trolley beside her. What the hell had they given him to make him so compliant? Nurses with green face masks worked in a brisk fashion not giving her so much as a second glance as she lay rigidly on her trolley. *"We come into this world alone and we leave it alone"* she thought morbidly, and indeed she had never felt so abandoned or in need of a reassuring hand to hold as she did now.

Swallowing hard, Serena tried to compose herself by practicing visualisation. *"You are going on a mind-blowing trip"* she told herself, *"you will float peacefully in a reassuringly warm ocean where gentle waves will lap against your entirely relaxed body."*

The dread moment had arrived. They were wheeling her towards the stainless-steel monster, Sebastian hovering anxiously beside her. Serena glimpsed the hateful tunnel where she would seamlessly slide inside, her body strapped firmly to the steel tray. Suffocating head straps with multiple wires attached would monitor the very core of her damaged brain. She screamed furiously but no words came out. The image of Edvard Munch's 'The Scream' flashed through her mind. She completely understood his angst. Pink Floyd's 'Wish You Were Here' was floating through the ER room's speakers; mood music for the stressed to pieces.

"I wish I were sodding anywhere but here," Serena thought bitterly. Tiny bright lights circled over her, and she felt the same helplessness and sickness as she did when she first entered the Channel Tunnel on her way to France. She was well and truly in the scanner now. The humming of the machine commenced, she wondered what the images of her brain were emitting to the doctors. Could they actually *see* what she was thinking?

"Fuck off" she told them silently. This was the worst experience of her life. She could feel tears prickling at the corners of her eyes. She concentrated harder than she had ever concentrated in her life. Harder than she had concentrated when she was given the order to 'Push as hard as you can' by the midwife, or 'Just do your best' by her father when tearfully contemplating a maths exam. Perhaps she had never concentrated hard enough; perhaps she didn't know how to. And this was her punishment, to feel absolutely wretched. But if she could find it in her to concentrate now…

Sebastian's hand slowly crept into hers. Her daughter Scarlett was laughing somewhere in the distance. She was lying on a smooth slatted wooden bench, sensing the motion of the sea. That was it, they were all on a boat together and she had lain down to savour the warmth of the sun, when his hand had crept into hers. His fingers felt long and slightly knobbly but wriggled gently and reassuringly against the palm of her hand. He still bit his nails badly. She must speak to him about that... The faint hum of the engine throbbed beneath them as the boat pushed gently forwards on its journey. 'I'm making my way to heaven' she thought, 'and who knew it would be so pleasant and easy?'

Making the mistake of opening her eyes, Serena came back to reality with a jolt... She was drenched in sweat, but slowly the steel tray underneath her started to slide and she was back in the familiar dark room again. A nurse was staring impassively at a control panel in the corner. A porter bent over her, stinking of cigarette smoke and she wrinkled her nose in distaste. 'Not dead yet then' she thought, as her eyes met Sebastian's. She smiled.

Back in her room a bossy, overweight and frankly unpleasant hospital administrator who had entered without knocking, stared at her maliciously. 'Your medical insurance hasn't been paid' she stated, baldly. Serena's euphoria at having survived the scanner evaporated in an instant. The thought of being presented with a bill running into thousands horrified her. She could clearly remember writing out the cheque and posting it, if not quite on time. She told the surly woman so. 'Nothing wrong with *your* brain then' the woman grunted. 'We'll have to check our records'.

Serena said nothing. 'How the hell did I end up here?' was her last conscious thought before a great weariness overtook her, and she fell asleep.

Freefall of Cocaine and Music

Drifting in and out of consciousness, Serena's first marriage swam into her mind as a freefall of cocaine and music, ending in misery.

Yet it had all begun so well.

Luke had been introduced to Serena by a mutual friend at a boozy Sunday lunch party. She found his wide smile and laid-back attitude to life instantly engaging. As she grew to know him, she realised that though was a gentle, kind and caring boyfriend, he was also something of a rebel. Her own adventurous heart warmed to this side of him. Luke had attended a repressive Catholic public school and had scandalised the priests by growing his curly hair down to his shoulders. He followed this by dropping out of University to turn his passion into a career; rock and roll.

Nevertheless, they married in a traditional Church service and Serena did the full-on 80s bride thing. The Vicar was only slightly taken aback when during the wedding rehearsal, Serena said 'Oh, I *love* this track' as Bach's Toccata and Fugue blared forth from Luke's ghetto-blaster.

Being married to someone in the forefront of the music business certainly had its advantages. Every weekday there would be a band to go and listen to. Most gigs were held at dark, crowded and slightly seedy small clubs, pulsating with loud music. They were huge fun, especially after a few pre-concert drinks to wash down a few pre-concert snorts. Serena could always identify the record label managers by their expensive suits, constant sniffs and clinging blonde PAs. In those days the industry had a real live pulse. It was exciting and vibrant; a heady mix of hard rock, punk, soul, New wave, New Romantics, funk, and jazz fusion. It was the 80s. People could choose to reinvent themselves overnight and many did. It was a fabulous, giddy yet dangerous era.

There were lots of perks or 'incentives' as they were classed. In other words, a never-ending supply of recreational drugs. In later years, whilst strongly condemning the use of any drugs whatsoever to her children, she would blushingly recall the bulging bags of white powder destined for a record launch party. A glass topped table had one use only. Anxious looking executives desperately trying to stay ahead of the game would pull thick wads of notes out of their pockets. If they were desperate, a bank note would already be tightly rolled.

Luke had once taken her to an album launch party hosted by a famous playboy, at his riverside mansion. So dumb and numbed were the band being celebrated, snorting and sniffing in their limo as they arrived, they completely failed to spot the hard-up hack lurking at the entrance to the estate. He got his picture.

Some fairly senior heads rolled the following week, as the storm broke with headlines screaming 'Playboy's Drug Den Busted' in a Sunday tabloid. 'Huh' thought Serena at the time. Soft drug use didn't shock her, and as far as she knew, heroin wasn't around. It had distressed her, though, to witness barely-of-age naked nymphets frolicking in fountains of cheap champagne. These young girls would openly ply their wares to the bug-eyed and drugged-up portly executives much to the annoyance of the industry PAs, whose sexual favours were often a passport to a much more exciting existence. The playboy nearly lost weekend custody of his children thanks to that

Serena was struggling with her day job at a highly fashionable West End advertising agency. Its open plan, uber-cool workspace was supposed to nurture the creative talent of the handsomely paid creative types. They would sit quietly in dreamy contemplation or take it in turns to throw hissy tantrums. Every Friday lunchtime, it was deemed that a full week's work had already been done. Black cabs would deposit employees at the sleek revolving red front doors as they fell haphazardly back into work after long boozy lunches. Having racked up huge expenses the indiscreet touting and hunting of drugs for the weekend would commence. Serena ignored the dealings but after one particularly strenuous session at an overpriced brasserie she succumbed to a quick line, simply to stay awake.

But then, totally off her head, she was gripped with an overwhelming desire to speak to her father, the man she trusted above all. She phoned his office number.

'He's in a board meeting' a flustered secretary responded.

'I must speak to him urgently' Serena insisted. When her father eventually came to the phone, he confirmed that he was hosting a meeting, but calmly asked her what he could do for her.

'I just needed to tell you that I love you' she said.

Though he must have realised that she was completely away with the fairies, he simply thanked her, and replied

'I love you too'.

Serena put the phone down, comforted that her father had an unconditional love for her that transcended everything. She would always remember and treasure that moment. For those few brief seconds it had just been the two of them and she knew that she would never have to question his love or doubt his sincerity. She imagined that all men would be strong, brave and loyal like her father.

Luke was a spoilt only child, born to a fairly staid couple late in life. 'Thank god he was a boy' her mother-in-law Edwina would say frequently. 'I would have groaned with despair had he been a girl'. Edwina was the daughter of a wealthy but feckless man who abandoned her at the Ritz Hotel in the late 40s, with enough money in stocks and shares to live independently. She was emotionally reserved but couldn't quite let go of her precious son and heir and could be competitive with Serena.

The couple lived in a blandly decorated house that Serena regarded as practical but dreary, the opposite of her own childhood home. On duty visits, Serena would be required to sit through kitchen suppers, always placed so that her eye would be drawn to the sign above the door. 'This is Edwina's kitchen. I am the BOSS'. And so she was. Her father-in-law was ten years older and seldom spoke much. She knew for example that he indulged in a scotch or two before supper and that he spent a lot of time at his golf club, but no other clues to his personality emerged.

Luke professed to love her with all his heart and when Sebastian was born, they were both thrilled. However, he took some risky business decisions and got into debt. Refusing to listen to legal advice, he put their London home up as security for a loan and when he defaulted on the payments, they lost everything. The house was repossessed and Serena, who was now pregnant with Scarlett, was forced to make decisions for all of them, as Luke seemed to shrink before her eyes.

They moved from London to Somerset, nearer to Serena's parents but Luke wasn't happy. Serena would always remember the look of horror on his face when he first witnessed her gardening at their tiny cottage. Donning a pair of wellingtons and a worn Barbour she had resolutely gripped her grandfather's fork. Its wooden handle was worn smooth by years of use and although slightly cracked she couldn't bear to part with it. Pushing its prongs firmly into the soil she lifted out a clod of earth shaking free the stones and making good the bed for vegetables. 'My heart is in the country' she told him happily, but sadly for them all, he felt quite differently.

Edwina was horrified when the marriage broke down. 'Whatever is the reason'? she had demanded of Serena. 'Luke doesn't love me any more" Serena replied simply. There was a momentary pause whilst Edwina thought about this. Her response was characteristically brisk and unemotional. 'Good Lord girl, you have two beautiful healthy children and you expect to be loved as well'?

Serena would never completely understand Luke's change of heart and that he could walk away from Sebastian and Scarlett. But she tried to respect the relationship between the children and Luke's parents. She made every effort to fit in with their timetable when they came to Somerset to visit but it was much harder when the children went to stay in London. The first time Luke had taken them away from her was for a four-day Easter break with his parents. Serena had only just finished breastfeeding Scarlett, who was only six months old. She couldn't really imagine Edwina soothing her baby, but Luke would not be dissuaded. When they left, she collapsed on the floor in grief. Those four days were pure hell as she yearned for her children, but there were many more separations to come.

At weekends Luke took them to a holiday home on a local estate where his parents sometimes joined them. The owners were an ambitious and successful couple at the top of their respective professions with children slightly older than Serena's. But there were tensions in their marriage and they constantly bickered. Sebastian and Scarlett would be deposited back to her bleary eyed and tired after these visits. They wanted quiet weekends spent in their own cosy home not forced intimacy with another family and stilted encounters with their grandparents. Bags of dirty linen would accompany their return as they thankfully settled into their own little safe space.

Waking briefly, Serena reflected that whether she liked it or not, these painful memories needed to be relived so that she could finally break free of them.

In the Country

Settling in to the community, Serena began to make friends. She had been divorced from Luke for a couple of years now and the children were happily ensconced at the local village school. Her neighbours Georgina and Charles, who lived at The Old Rectory, welcomed her into their home with a generosity that she could never hope to return. So when Georgina suggested that she volunteer as a beater at the local shoot to keep her company, she happily agreed. Though she hadn't a gun dog, her enthusiasm cheered up the small shoot on a sodden day. The two friends did nothing but laugh as they beat their way through thick damp undergrowth or tapped the bare branches of the hedgerows with their sticks whilst surveying the beauty of the countryside.

Georgina had a pair of glossy black labradors at whom she would bellow 'Come back here NOW' in crystal-clear upper-class vowels as she trained them to retrieve. 'For Christ's sake' she would mutter after a hard drive 'Pass me the bloody hip flask'. The engraved silver vessel would be passed between them. 'Charles's family crest'? Serena once enquired, eyebrows raised quizzically. To the bemusement of the other beaters more snorts of laughter followed.

The guns were a mixed bunch of local farmers who would arrive in muddy pick-up trucks with border collies barking furiously from the back. They held their trousers up with bale twine in stark contrast to the casually yet carefully attired local gentry. In those days, shoots were good fun and open to all. Later on, they began to cater for the *nouveau riche* who would arrive in helicopters and be dressed from head to toe in impeccable tweeds. As well as being an extraordinary loyal friend, Georgina had the added attraction of an eligible older brother. Serena tried to feign serious disinterest in Robin, a strapping Gloucestershire farmer with the naughtiest twinkle in his eye. He would ruffle her hair in a friendly fashion, then lift her off her feet and envelop her in an enormous bear hug. The most she ever achieved was a champagne fuelled kiss after a family christening in the walled garden of the Rectory. She later learnt she wasn't the only one. She supposed that a newly divorced woman with two small children surviving virtually hand to mouth in a tiny cottage was hardly likely to turn his handsome head. Nor would she join the queue of his admirers, so that was that. Years later, when her life had moved on, they would regularly sit next to each other at Georgina's cheerful dinner parties. The wine would flow, and they would flirt outrageously, much to the annoyance of whatever girlfriend he had brought along (he never married). She thought it was time to confess to him that she had once thought him utterly delectable.

'How extraordinary' he had replied, ' I thought you were too'. But in her heart, she knew it would have been a hopeless match.

Randolph makes an Appearance

During one shoot, Serena met the county set's blacksmith Fergus, perhaps a little too rough and ready for her taste, but one of the few eligible bachelors in the neighbourhood. He had casually mentioned that he was looking for a 'couple of birds' to join him and a newly separated friend for supper that night. Serena was unimpressed but when she mentioned it to her parents, they urged her to go out.

'It'll do you good' they said firmly, and duly arrived that evening for babysitting services. If nothing else, the invitation seemed a good opportunity to don her latest charity shop purchase, a navy-blue wool and cashmere trench coat, but otherwise, her expectations were low. Her single friend Sarah had agreed to make up the numbers but fretted all the way there.

'It's not right and proper' she bemoaned 'to go to supper with people that I haven't even been introduced to.' Serena was bored before she even stepped out of the car.

Fergus's cottage lay on a slight hill on the outskirts of a tiny village. That night it was surrounded by ghostly, swirling Dorset mists. The gravel drive crunched loudly as they pulled up and his gun dogs began a furious cacophony of barking. Despite being comfortably off, Fergus was known for being careful with money. Serena guessed the chunky gravel had been the cheaper option for the drive, but she risked wrecking her precious high heels as she picked her way to the front door.

The smell of wet dog hit them as soon as they stepped inside the cold narrow kitchen, a crudely tacked on extension to the original building. Fergus was wearing one of his many rough checked work shirts and looked faintly uncomfortable.

'This is Randolph, ladies' and Serena and Sarah turned to see a tall, distinguished looking man wielding a large sharp cooking knife. A more interesting proposition than she had expected, thought Serena, as they shook hands. Never one to show that she was impressed, she stood there in her second-hand attire and haughtily looked him up and down.

Randolph was every inch the aristocratic eccentric. Lean, languid and possessing a large aquiline nose, he nonchalantly took a long luxurious appraisal of Serena and Sarah as they were ushered through into the drawing room. He wore the obligatory sand coloured cords only his were far too short for his long legs. An old navy blue and red woollen pullover that had seen better days covered a Jermyn street shirt, fraying at the collar. Gold cufflinks with the family coat of arms discreetly peered out. His English public-school education had nearly eradicated his Russian origins, but a slight accent could still be detected behind the slow, upper-class drawl. The effect was almost hypnotic.

Sarah quickly offered to help him in the kitchen, eagerly chopping up vegetables for the fish *bouillabaisse* he was cooking, to be followed by rabbit cooked in a creamy white sauce. Randolph was clearly fully aware of the seductive charm of a man who is at home in the kitchen. Turning to a flustered Fergus, who was burdened which coats, he announced:

'We're all dying for a drink', which lightened the suddenly charged atmosphere.

For three of the party this was a first-time introduction, so they took their drinks gratefully and sat down at the small pine dining-table, on heavy and uncomfortable chairs. Within a couple of hours, the conversation was animated and bright. It seemed that another glass or two would not go amiss. There was an awkward pause. Randolph looked pointedly at Fergus who simply shrugged his shoulders. Expressing incredulity at his host's parsimonious offering of one bottle of wine Randolph pointed out that were it not for the fact the ladies had each politely come bearing gifts that it would have been a mean and wretchedly dry evening.

'You must have a bottle somewhere surely'? he protested. Silence reigned whilst Serena pondered where a canny Scotsman might hide a bottle or two. She rose from the table and went straight to the unlit fire, reaching up the wide chimney breast. Her instincts proved to be spot on and she returned to the table brandishing a bottle of whiskey much to Fergus's discomfort. He feebly protested that he had forgotten it was there, arguing that 'deal' between himself and Randolph was that he would provide the female company and his friend would provide the food.

'And *you* didn't bring a bottle did you'? he spat accusingly at Randolph.

'I'm locked out of my bloody cellar at present as you damn well know' was the curt reply. After pacifying himself with a slug of whiskey Fergus retorted that he didn't know what all the fuss was about.

'They're only a couple of 'pudding girls' after all, he sniggered, 'not exactly top drawer'. Serena stiffened. Sarah, who very much placed herself in the top drawer was singularly unamused. Having downsized from a substantial estate after an ugly divorce, she was struggling to adjust to her straitened circumstances and her mouth set in a tight line. Serena herself had never professed to be anything other than middle-class. Having encountered a ghastly selection of snobs one way or another, she knew that well-bred people never judge a person by their background, but purely on their hearts, minds and manners. She had noticed that the newly rich tended to come a cropper in just the social circles they wished to belong to, by attempting to be something they were not, and she prided herself on her own lack of pretension. However, she thought the less of Fergus for his snobbery. Randolph changed the subject.

They all hovered over coffee, as the evening drew to a close.

'I'll just pop to the loo' Serena said and was shown to a lightweight wooden door with a flimsy latch which led up to narrow steep stairs. A frayed and insubstantial carpet covered the poorly-lit stairwell. On the second stair was a solitary toothbrush with a half-squeezed tube of toothpaste. Randolph must be staying the night then. A blast of cold air hit her as she entered the bathroom. She was taken aback by its starkness and the flimsy old-fashioned curtains that hung at the windows. It wasn't the sort of room you would choose to linger in. She noticed the razor and the grubby shaving soap with its worn bristle brush standing on the cracked white porcelain sink. What a miserable bachelor pad, she thought to herself. Slightly flushed faces turned towards her as she re-joined the group. There was a momentarily shuffling of feet under the table and an embarrassed pause hung in the air.

'Perhaps we should all meet again' someone suggested. It transpired that it was Fergus's birthday the following week and he proposed they all meet for lunch somewhere. Serena knew there was a special offer running at the local country house hotel, so she suggested this. This was greeted by tremendous enthusiasm by all and she was secretly pleased by her quick thinking.

The following week found the two women rolling up the steeply gravelled drive once more. Randolph and Fergus both looked quite dapper Serena noted. It was decided they take two cars as Randolph had to depart early to do a school run. 'So, he has children, does he?' thought Serena, as she made a beeline for Fergus's car, forcing Sarah to climb into Randolph's car. It was blindingly obvious she was rather taken with him, whereas Serena thought him rather old in comparison to Robin, of whom she was still dolly-daydreaming.

They started off down the beautiful winding lanes. Fergus had his foot on the accelerator and they laughed easily in each other's company. They soon left the others behind. Suddenly he stopped at a humpbacked bridge and pointed down at the gentle banks sloping into a tranquil stream. It was a private spot hidden from view.

'I once made love down there', he confessed, giving a slightly embarrassed laugh and looking at her sideways as if to gauge her reaction. It was instantaneous, they both dissolved into loud giggles and when they spied the other two in the rear-view mirror, they set off again quickly.

The Lodge was everything a comfortable country house should be. Snugly tucked away and enveloped by deepest Dorset countryside it oozed comfort and an escape from everyday life. The open log fire smouldered reassuringly as the sunlight filtered through the windows of the elegant drawing room. They all settled into the homely spacious sofas clad in a classic William Morris fabric and studied the menus. Randolph was wearing a tweed herringbone suit which, although it had seen better days and bore leather trim at the cuffs, still cut a dash. Another thick stripy Jermyn street shirt completed the laid-back upper-class *ensemble*.

Looking away from Randolph, Serena surveyed the other diners, gently sipping their *aperitifs*. Ladies with slim elegantly crossed legs chatted with husbands or lovers with newly shaven faces and suits that rarely saw the light of day. A couple were cosied up close together and were quite obviously staying.

Serena and friends were all on the fixed price menu, however. The pork looked good and they gave their orders to the young waiter hovering beside them, eager to please.

'Exactly what breed of pig is the pork'? Randolph enquired. Serena was amazed that the waiter, though surprised, immediately hurried off to find out. A couple of moments later the waiter returned and stuttered shyly: 'The pork is Berkshire Old Spot, sir'.

'Absolutely splendid' drawled Randolph, scarcely giving the young man a second glance. 'Oh, I adore Berkshire pork' Sarah piped up brightly. She clearly prided herself on being a foodie and engaged Randolph in a lively discussion of rare piggy breeds. Serena secretly thought they were being rather pretentious but wisely kept her counsel. Instead, once they were seated at their table, she told them that the proprietor's wife did all the lavish flower arrangements herself, having trained at Constance Spry. This effectively conveyed the impression that she dined here regularly, and Sarah quietened down a trifle.

A perfectly cooked lunch worked its emollient magic and they all had a great deal of fun. Handsome thick cream menus with the date lay discarded on the table. 'I don't believe I have the ladies' phone numbers' Randolph stated, with a mischievous look in his eye. Sarah giggled nervously and discreetly scribbled down her number. Serena was bolder. She pulled out her Montblanc fountain pen – a cherished relic from her wealthier days – and wrote her name and number in a looped, artistic scrawl.

As they sat enjoying a cup of coffee by the dying embers of the fire, they started to discuss thermal underwear; it was rather cold after all. Randolph raised his eyebrows mockingly and his eyes met Serena's blandly.

'Underwear'? The word hung provocatively in the air. 'I don't believe I've remembered to put any on'. They all roared with laughter.

Later, when Serena turned up at the village school to pick up her children a few of the mother's remarked on her smart clothes. 'I've been out to lunch' she informed them and readily agreed to assist with the school's Christmas tombola. She drove home thinking how lucky she was to have new friends to occupy her thoughts, rather than simply being a lone parent to two small children,

The Cottage

A couple of days later, Serena was idly warming her bottom against her old cream Rayburn and day-dreaming again when the phone rang.

'Hello' a voice drawled, 'it's me'.

Surprised though she was to hear from Randolph, part of her thought 'Hmm, a tad arrogant of him to assume that I would recognise his voice… but then it was pretty distinctive'. Randolph said how much he had enjoyed lunch at The Lodge and she agreed that it had been a resounding success. After a while he hesitated, and after a pregnant pause said simply:

'I rather like you'.

Serena was momentarily silenced by this remark, which struck her as a rather forward. And its absurdity struck her immediately. 'But we're complete opposites' she stammered 'so that's a ridiculous remark'. There was a pause, and then he retorted

'Opposites attract' and put down the phone.

The Christmas tree, resplendent in all its festive finery stood opposite her as she plonked herself down on the sofa laughing to herself. The promise of interesting days ahead seemed to cling to its glittery branches. 'Maybe next year won't be so bad', she mused.

On the last shoot before the holidays hip flasks were *de rigeur* for everyone in the icy cold. More slugging than beating occurred but the brisk walk gave Serena a rosy glow. Randolph suddenly materialised amongst the guns. A rather dated silk cravat was knotted round his neck. Serena had never liked cravats and she didn't approve of his dark green Grenfell jacket, so she merely nodded at him, and stuck close to Georgina, hoping to bring the conversation round to Robin. Randolph and his cravat really weren't her style.

At the end of the day she was presented with a brace of pheasant and a bloodied rabbit dangling on string. Anxious to get home and warm up, she was irritated when Randolph appeared by her side. The rabbit was dripping blood onto the bonnet of her car leaving a sticky trail down the side. 'I daresay' the familiar voice said, 'that you'll be needing some assistance skinning this, I'll pop by later'. And without giving her time to reply, he strolled away.

Sebastian and Scarlett came home from school and eyed the dangling dead bodies with fascination. Just as Serena was deciding to claim that the cat next door had slunk off with the rabbit, there was sharp rap on the door knocker. Both children scurried up the narrow flight of wooden stairs and from the safety of their hiding place peered down at the unfamiliar figure. Randolph's great height seemed to fill the tiny kitchen. He deftly unhooked the creature and requesting some newspaper from a discombobulated Serena, set to work. Using a sharp army knife, he slit the rabbit from its rear end to its neck and pulled off its skin like a jacket over its head. By this time two pairs of small eyes were riveted by the unprecedented scene

Playing to the gallery, Randolph placed his fingers into the skin and did an impromptu puppet show, much to the children's delight. 'Pop it into the fridge' he ordered, as he prepared to leave 'and we'll have it for supper tomorrow night. I'll call Fergus and Sarah'. Weak with relief that the wretched thing had been efficiently dealt with, Serena felt she had no option but to agree.

The next day found her poring through her cookbooks for the best recipe for rabbit stew. The ancient and slightly chipped Rayburn would ensure it was cooked slowly and despite some qualms, she found herself rather looking forward to entertaining for a change. It was a good excuse to pop on some heels, apply some lipstick and enjoy adult company. The dark evenings could be rather lonely although the cosy cottage really was at its finest in the winter months. She loved sitting by a log fire in the inglenook fireplace that her father had discovered behind a bricked-up wall. Even when alone, she lit flickering candles on the original wide wooden shelf above. A dining table was squeezed into the corner of the sitting-room, battling for space with the tree. Her father had been brilliant helping her renovate the cottage and had built a window seat for them. The décor would be described as 'shabby chic' but because she hadn't any money, the choice of style was forced rather than chosen. When Luke had gone bankrupt and they had lost their London home, a friend had lent her the money to buy the cottage which was deemed 'uninhabitable' by the local council. As Serena was pregnant with Scarlett, they desperately needed somewhere affordable and she was fully alive to the cottage's potential. Luke appeared to be paralysed by his misfortune and went along with her plans, seemingly happily. An elderly lady had lived there previously, and the council had done some insensitive additions such as fitting a downstairs loo by ripping through the old flagstones. Up until then the inhabitants had used an old dunny situated down the garden.

Sebastian was given a room which was just about large enough to hold bunk beds, the thin wooden wall between him and the staircase rattled every time small people excitedly rushed up and down. Scarlett's bedroom was off Serena's with a flying freehold over the cottage next door. All that separated them from the neighbours was a locked door. Fortunately, they shared this arrangement with a couple of confirmed bachelors who were twins and regarded Serena's renovations with quiet amusement. The first time Georgina and Charles came round, Charles rather absentmindedly went to carry on through the cottage via the back door, assuming that it was far larger. When confronted with a pitch-black garden he looked rather startled. 'Good Lord' he exclaimed 'is this where you live'?

But it had charm. Serena's father had cleverly burnt the name 'The Cottage' into a piece of driftwood from the beach and a tiny black fox-head knocker found at a jumble sale completed the quaint front door's welcoming look. The only residual problem were the mice, who would sometimes scurry across the living room floor at night. The council's pest control expert could not have been kinder as he dealt with the problem, regaling her with horror stories of elderly clients unknowingly living alongside actual *rats*. Yet the bastard mice still tormented her, scurrying above her head as they scratched the flimsy ceiling of the attic above her bedroom. She had imagined them gnawing their way through what was not much more than thick board and would anxiously watch the trapdoor above her head for signs of beady brown eyes…

But that evening, she thought with satisfaction, her sitting-room looked welcoming and festive. Two newly-bathed and pyjama-clad children, sat happily by the fire, intrigued by the novelty of the situation. When she heard voices at the front door, Serena stepped briskly forward, saying over her shoulder 'Here we go!'.

From the pitch-black lane outside, Sarah stepped into the kitchen first. 'Goodness, isn't this sweet!' she exclaimed. She could hardly say anything else; she might have been forced to downsize but was still living in a fairly substantial property. Fergus entered next, wearing the same shirt as the first evening, but (happily) clutching a bottle. Lastly, Randolph came stooping through the doorway, resplendent in a rich dark blue velvet jacket with a matching silk bow-tie. Blinking at this plumage, Serena initially failed to notice that he had a dead squirrel hanging down the sides of his mouth, like a grotesque distorted moustache. He whipped it off quickly.

'Nothing like a touch of squirrel to liven up a bunny stew' he quipped. Was he being serious? It was difficult to tell. 'I don't think so, thank you' she ventured rather primly, horrified that it might end up in the pot. Grinning, he hung it nonchalantly on the hook between the kitchen and the downstairs bathroom. Sarah squealed loudly and backed away in horror. This was just the reaction he was looking for. The children sat rigid on the sofa, in horrified fascination. Who *was* this most peculiar man?

Serena knew with a sinking heart that the incident would get straight back to Luke and their grandparents, and that Luke was unlikely to be amused. She would be cross questioned on the suitability of the joke. Yet despite its inauspicious beginning, the evening was a roaring success, and Serena went to bed happy in the knowledge that her humble home had sparkled.

Serena had the now awkward Christmas gathering to look forward to. Since her separation a pattern had been set. Luke would arrive with his mother in tow and rather like a grand duchess she would critically survey her precious grand-children's environment and cross-question Serena on their general development. Serena's parents would drive over, bringing a turkey they had cooked in their larger oven. They would all be falsely, but impeccably polite to each other, striving to look like a united family for the sake of the children. It was the cruellest day of the year for Serena, bringing home with complete clarity how things should have been. After a couple of glasses of champagne, she always felt tearful as she struggled to cope. Had she let them all down by abandoning London and embracing the countryside? She knew that Luke thought this. But when they had lost their London home because of his business debts, she instinctively wanted to be near her parents whilst she licked her wounds. She blamed herself, still too raw to recognise that Luke could have adapted to a rural life for the sake of his children.

Money - or rather the lack of - it brought about by Luke's over-ambitious plans was the main reason for the breakdown of the marriage. Serena had never experienced money worries before. She had trusted Luke implicitly, so it had hit her hard when it had all gone wrong. She also blamed herself for not keeping an eye on his business activities, but then Sebastian had been so tiny. She sighed, as she contemplated the washing up to be done later...

Randolph had invited himself round the previous evening with a bottle of champagne, but the fireplace was smoking so badly it was difficult to see across the room. Consequently, she had woken on Christmas morning with red rimmed eyes. Not a great start to the day, she had thought bitterly. Despite the champagne, after Randolph had left, she had felt dispirited. It was an emotionally charged business wrapping carefully chosen presents on her own. After stuffing the goodies into two woollen socks she had tiptoed upstairs and hung them at the end of the children's beds. Looking down on them both sleeping so peacefully she had felt the familiar mixture of sadness and regret.

Randolph's Soirée

Randolph had rented a small cottage on the coast from some friends who were away for the holidays. Having seen his own children briefly, for reasons which he expertly glossed over, he had spent Christmas day itself with Sarah's family. Now he had arranged another supper party in the no man's land between Christmas and New Year. Serena was free to attend since the children were spending a couple of days with Luke. It was bitterly cold; the only hint of warmth came from a meanly-sized fireplace in the corner. Sarah seemed oddly expectant, for reasons that were unclear to Serena. Randolph as usual stole the show in the fashion stakes by sporting a very tight and flimsy pair of white silk trousers, more suited to the tropics than freezing Dorset. It was blindingly obvious that once again he had forgotten to put on any underwear.

A plate of oysters was proffered along with a glass of chilled champagne. Though Serena enjoyed watching the tiny bubbles rise majestically to the top of her glass there was a very strange atmosphere. Randolph seemed irritated with Sarah who was shucking down oysters as fast as she could. When she made a disparaging remark about the size of the shellfish, Randolph cuttingly told her that she was acting in a vulgar fashion 'more in keeping with the uneducated and ill-informed middle classes'. Her face twitched with fury, but then something caught her eye and she screamed.

'It's a rat' she spluttered, pointing her finger accusingly at a harmless old hamster lumbering along slowly on his old wheel. This lightened the mood and they all fell about laughing. Randolph refilled their glasses with a flourish. Serena couldn't recall what they ate after that, because there were sexually-charged undercurrents in the room. Subtle flirtations were taking place as they all sat huddled on the inadequate sofa. Unusually, she was wearing a very tight black dress which became indecently short when she sat back. She stood up to adjust it, and when she sat down again, she felt fingers wriggling expertly against her bottom, and yelped indignantly. Fergus and Sarah looked extremely disapproving. Excusing herself, Serena asked the way to the loo. 'I'll show you; it's very dark' said Randolph as he followed her into the kitchen. The other two, deeply suspicious of Randolph's motives were close behind him. Stumbling into a damp and dated bathroom, searching for the light switch, she thought instantly of her own warm bathroom, filled with brightly coloured children's toys. Suddenly, a pair of hands grabbed her round the waist. Randolph had cheekily sneaked in after her and locked the door behind him. Before she realised what he intended, he had spun her towards him and fastened his mouth on hers. She was being kissed! And extremely passionately, too. She had drunk enough champagne not to rebuff the advance although the other two were banging on the door. She emerged rather sheepishly but not without noticing he had a rather toned pair of buttocks.

The division of the foursome had obviously been decided with Sarah and Fergus announcing that they were going home. Serena hesitated fractionally, as Randolph went to get their coats. Noticing this, Fergus hissed in her ear: 'You can either stay here or have a lift home, although I feel it my duty to inform you that Randolph is a serial womaniser with a reputation in quite a few counties.'

That did it. Serena was no easy conquest, although she would have been perfectly entitled to stay without any guilt. After all, she was single. (She later realized that married women were far more to Randolph's taste). But she accepted Fergus's offer. Sarah seemed agitated, but Serena couldn't figure out why. Perhaps she was still cross about being called vulgar? It didn't occur to her that Sarah might be put out for other reasons.

Fergus dropped them off at Sarah's house, declining to come in for a nightcap, and after resurrecting a smouldering fire, she suggested they have some more champagne. It wasn't long before the effects of the extra bubbly started to kick in. 'So' Sarah began, 'you and Randolph, smooching in the bathroom; have you got your eye on him'? Serena thought about this hazily but before she could reply, Sarah wagged a finger. 'I have to tell you' Sarah continued conspiratorially, 'that he made a pass at me on Christmas day and hinted very heavily that he would like to stay the night'. She looked challengingly at Serena to gauge her reaction.

'Be my guest' Serena told her, 'I'm simply not interested'.

Half an hour later, she called a cab and escaped to the sanctuary of her own home.

Nevertheless, and rather to her surprise, a few days later she found herself once more down at the tiny cottage, with a promise of lunch at the local pub. It was a wintry grey afternoon, the children were having a sleepover with some friends, and she didn't have anything better to do. Randolph looked rather pleased with himself.

'I've rescued my cellar' he explained, as he pulled a cork from an impressive looking bottle of Burgundy. 'Red burgundy comes from the eastern region of France' he explained 'using one hundred per cent *pinot noir* grapes. They are some of the most expensive wines in the world. What makes them so special is that they are completely influenced by the *terroir* giving them a unique quality that is very specific to each individual vineyard'. Serena listened intently; she was always eager to learn new things.

'This is a *premier cru* rather than a *grand cru*. Maybe when we get to know each other better I will share one of those grander bottles with you'. 'Sniff it first' he instructed 'then sip it slowly. What are your first thoughts'?

They carried on like this for a while until he told her to 'quaff up before the wine goes off and the taste changes dramatically'. They moved on to another bottle. Serena found the pop of a cork being pulled on an expensive vintage very pleasing. However before long, their thoughts began to turn to food, so they walked in a leisurely, slightly drunken fashion to the pub. A few locals sat huddled at the bar but other than that they were alone in the dining area. An uninspiring menu was chalked on a blackboard, but the charge between them was so exhilarating that the quality of the food was immaterial.

Several hours later, Serena reflected how unsettling it was to be lying next to a strange man. For one thing, he was fifteen years her senior. His hair was grey and thinning, in complete contrast to Luke's abundant locks and she wasn't entirely comfortable with that. However here she was, for good or ill, and the wine was certainly helping...

Afterwards, she shed a few tears but didn't know whether it was from relief that she was still desirable or some deeper emotion. When she propped herself up on the pillows and looked out of the window, the sky held a yellowish tinge above the single-track lane outside. 'Oh well, too late to worry now' she reasoned and turning her face to the pillow, she fell asleep effectively snuffing out any further thoughts.

In the early days of their relationship, Randolph hardly ever mentioned his family and preoccupied with her own children, Serena wasn't initially interested. But his mobile would ring at all hours, and she couldn't avoid noticing that many of them were from an hysterical sounding woman. It all sounded terribly complicated.

Eventually she asked him 'How many children do you have'?

'Eight' he replied briskly, 'although whether I have sired them all is anyone's guess'. She was shocked, but this was just the first of the many vicious accusations he levelled at his wife, from whom he was separated. At the time, he seemed completely plausible. Had Serena thought a little more deeply or stepped back a trifle, she might have wondered exactly why he was so estranged from his children. As it was, she only saw what she wanted to see; that an intelligent, witty and unusual man was interested in her.

She also ignored some clues which in hindsight, were obvious. The empty father Christmas sack still containing extravagant wrapping paper with cryptic messages in female handwriting. 'From a very dear old friend' he explained, blandly. On another occasion, a neat wicker basket stood by the back door of his rented cottage. It contained an empty bottle of vintage champagne and packaging that had contained an assortment of delicacies. The writing on the basket's label was different. 'I'm fortunate to have such generous friends' he said. Eventually, he told her that these female admirers were married to well-known and respected local men of some standing. She should have sensed the hopelessness of a relationship with such a man but to her eternal regret, did not.

January

They continued to see each other. If Serena's parents were horrified, they didn't say so. It must have been blindingly obvious to them that she was making a terrible mistake.

Early one morning, Randolph announced they were going on a walk. After driving for a while, he parked, and led her into a field. A house emerged in the distance through the flimsy dispersing mist, as the sun tried to break through. Its boundary was marked by low stone walls smothered in moss and lichen. She could see formal, ornate gardens and a pond with a fountain pushing up delicate sprays of water. She guessed there would be a wealth of fish lurking under expansive lush greenery and imagined their bulky shapes moving gracefully under the water. By contrast, the house looked completely closed and unloved. They came to a wooden gate leading to a field full of sheep grazing peacefully, and she stared at the house from this nearer prospect.

'Bloody hell' she said 'look at that place, I wonder who lives there'.

'I do' Randolph replied 'or rather I did. It's my house'.

After a quick glance at his inscrutable expression, Serena transferred her gaze to the muddy path ahead, although her mind was racing. The cottage he was now renting was filled with black plastic crates full of unopened mail. He had given her the keys whilst he went on one of his occasional trips to London, asking her to pop in to ensure the heating was on. 'Just a small favour' he begged. When she went around to do that, she was shocked by the unkempt and stark surroundings. She set to, tidying away a copious amount of paperwork and when he let himself in, there was a merry fire blazing away. All the paperwork had needed dealing with as a matter of urgency. Randolph, she discovered over the years, was incapable of coping with official documents, particularly from his creditors. He simply preferred to put his head in the sand and pretend it wasn't happening, neatly sidestepping the issue and leaving the mess for someone else to deal with. She guessed that his financial position was rocky and that his divorce would be hugely acrimonious.

His barren cottage aside, Randolph put on a convincing front. He grandly went along to his club in London, unable to give up all the trappings that went with a certain degree of wealth and privilege. In his trinket box were a few tantalizing objects that hinted at a mysterious past. He would regale anyone who would listen with stories about his family's supposedly royal connections. He hinted at intrigue and mystery. He was never happier than obligingly playing to an audience captivated by the impossibility of it all and easily impressed. And he played to perfection the hapless victim suffering at the hands of an abusive wife, claiming that she had tried to kill him. Yet one of his most treasured possessions was a beret bearing the SAS badge. He had never served, was only in the reserve but it didn't occur to Serena that someone with SAS training was scarcely likely to live in fear of his wife.

Possibly Serena didn't notice certain anomalies because she was busy trying to survive on the pittance Luke gave her. He was leading the life of a single man in London, free of the day-to-day responsibilities of two small children. To help make ends meet, she did a part time cleaning job for one of the guns on the shoot. A vet by profession, obsessively clean by nature, it wasn't an arduous way to pull in a few extra pounds. Forming part of an old stable conversion, Serena thought his house functional, and lacking a feminine touch. Though she did occasionally dolly daydream about how life would be for them all if they had such an abundance of space, the classically good-looking vet did nothing for her. A friend called Carol came to help in theory but mostly to relieve the boredom of having nothing much to clean during her appointed hours.

Carol knew Randolph, since her husband rented out some of the farmland which surrounded his former house. She was a large boned, dark-haired striking woman and not adverse to pushing out her voluptuous bosom whilst claiming to be a black witch. Serena found her rather fascinating and wasn't in the least bit intimidated by her. They would both shriek with laughter at ridiculously small things as they worked alongside each other. One day she came up very close to Serena, her face inches away, with a slight smirk on her face.

'Do you want to know a secret' she hissed. Serena thought she probably did.

'I gave Randolph a massage the other day', she said, lowering her voice further so that Serena had to strain forward to hear her. She elaborated. 'A slow, sensual massage', she continued, emphasising each syllable of 'sensual'. Serena's throat constricted, but she forced a smile.

'When he turned over, he had a right hard on, I can tell you'. She was now practically touching Serena's face with hers. For a mad moment, a repulsed Serena thought Carol was about to try and kiss her, but she stood her ground. Carol sucked her teeth and grinned lasciviously as she added 'I said he could just take me right there and then, if he chose'.

Serena stared at the woman incredulously. Surely Randolph had not made a pass at this rather coarse woman, with her thick wild tangled hair and bizarre dress sense? She should have paid more heed.

Randolph Moves On

Randolph announced he was moving into Fergus's cottage, although he was spending more and more time with Serena.

'Why pay for a whole house'? he maintained 'when now I simply have to pay for one bedroom which I shall hardly ever use anyway? I only need a postal address, just to keep up appearances'.

Fergus, however, was uneasy. He took Serena aside. 'You do know he's about to run out of money, don't you? He has the most monumental debts.'

Serena thought this was extremely disloyal of Fergus. By then, Randolph had thoroughly bewitched her. Stuck in a tiny cottage and craving adult company, she found his culinary skills and attentive manner equally irresistible. When he suggested it, she agreed to let him move in with them. She wouldn't admit it, but she had been lonely. Rural life was grand when you had someone to share its ups and downs with. All but a few of Randolph's wealthy university friends had abandoned him in his misfortunes. He made it clear that he needed both her company and emotional support. And together they built a small social circle. She would witness people sitting spellbound and engrossed as he effortlessly held court. She was later to discover that beneath his anecdotes were secrets and lies that went with him to his grave.

Soon after he moved in, when the promise of spring hung in the air, Randolph announced he was going to his former home. He begged Serena to go too, and she agreed, although she couldn't understand why he was so uptight about the visit. He knew that his estranged wife was away, so there was no risk of confrontation.

Driving up an imposing tree-lined avenue, a stream and a three-bar wooden fence to one side, the house came into view. Parking, they looked at the deserted building in silence. A neighbour out walking his dog looked at Randolph with ill-disguised curiosity. There was no dirty laundry that had not been publicly aired for all to chew over. The solid and traditional house stood resolutely alone. Large windows with drapes tightly closed kept out prying eyes. An air of melancholy and sadness wrapped itself around the red bricks of the facade. Serena felt uneasy, but Randolph was insistent that it was his home containing all his family heirlooms, and he had every right to be there. Even so, Serena entered the house without enthusiasm. She blinked as they went through the front door into total darkness. All the interior wooden shutters had also been closed shrouding the rooms in gloom and ensuing even the merest fraction of light could not enter.

A doorway in the corner led into a kitchen which had marble topped surfaces, and wall-to-wall pale grey painted units. It was spotlessly tidy. 'She can't cook' Randolph snorted, 'I doubt the room ever gets used'. In the middle island sat a vast arrangement of dying lilies in a heavy, clear glass vase.

In other rooms, dark and heavy antique furniture sat on brightly coloured Persian rugs. Numerous stern portraits hung on the walls. 'They're all of my family' Randolph announced rather grimly. He moved in an agitated fashion towards some pictures in silver frames on a lighter, and altogether more handsome chest of drawers. A jumbled group peered into the camera posing happily on a quayside. In the background were the distinctive shapes of brightly coloured sails, outlined against a searing blue sky.

'Cannes?' ventured Serena.

'One of her ex-lovers' haunts' came the curt reply. 'I was left behind mopping up yet another of my sister's sordid divorces'.

Serena was surprised; Randolph hadn't mentioned the existence of a sister before. But perhaps they weren't close. As if reading Serena's thoughts, he told her that his sister was 'as mad as a hatter' although he would later concede that his parents had been cruel to her, forcing her to sit upright at mealtimes with a coat hanger in her blouse, to correct her posture. He snatched up another picture and stuffed it into his jacket pocket. 'I *am* allowed one miserable picture of my family, surely?'

He couldn't keep the bitterness out of his voice and much to Serena's relief, they left the house. He then began to tell her stories about the people in his social circle. Who was having an affair with whom, and tales of abortions necessitated by impregnations from forbidden lovers. This or that person was currently undergoing therapy for drug/drink addictions; he seemed determined to shock her and he succeeded. To an outsider, this other world of his, apparently one of wealth and privilege, now seemed distinctly seedy. She imagined them as a mass of poisonous vipers, writhing and slithering over each other in their quest for extra sexual gratification in the county set. Randolph, she later learnt was no better. He simply couldn't keep his pants zipped up, such was the thrill of seducing other people's wives.

Fergus had, after all, tried to warn her off, although she subsequently felt he might have tried a bit harder. If he had told her even a few stories of dalliances, she might have listened. Randolph had often been the recipient of expensive gifts from a so-called former lover when staying with Fergus. But he would airily deny that they meant anything. Some years later, Serena bumped into the woman herself and without emotion told her that she had had a narrow escape. She laughed nervously as she took in Serena's words.

'I hardly think so' she eventually said in a faltering voice, 'I am married, after all' and she shrugged off Serena's comment with a self-satisfied smile.

'You omitted the word happily' Serena retorted and had to restrain herself from further comment. She was to wish that she had encouraged the woman to carry on with Randolph instead of insisting that he cut the connection. That would have been that, and she would have escaped, narrowly. They would have all been spared so much pain. If only...

Dubai and Polite Society

A generous cousin of Serena's gave her a ticket to join her in Dubai, alone. It was the first time she had left the children for any length of time and they were to go to their grandparents, leaving Randolph with the complete run of her home.

The thought of this did make her rather uneasy. Stories of his escapades in London had got back to her, and she had seen table napkins from smart restaurants containing hastily scrawled phone numbers. Used match boxes heavily embossed with the logos of various gentleman's clubs lay scattered on his bedside table. In those days the only way to stay in touch with the children and Randolph was by fax or telephone. Fax was much the cheapest, and the children would send her lovely letters telling her about their daily doings. Randolph bombarded her with declarations of love and images of the palm of his hand outstretched. A couple of hours later would come the written confession that he was hosting a small dinner party. 'Only a little social gathering' he protested, 'you wouldn't want me sitting here all on my own now would you'? It seemed churlish at the time to object or complain.

Once back from Dubai, Serena felt more resilient than she had in a long while. Luke's bankruptcy and the shock of the divorce had robbed her of her natural self-confidence. She had acquired a tan, and enjoyed a lively time being wined and dined by the ex-pat crowd as they amused themselves amidst the false glitter of a city built on shifting sand. It was a welcome change to be surrounded by monied people whose sole purpose in life was to have some fun and live for the moment.

Sensing that she'd enjoyed her taste of the good life, Randolph realised that he needed to up his game. He announced, somewhat patronisingly, that Serena was now fit to be introduced to 'polite society'. He took her to meet two of his oldest friends who were at one of their several properties, a picture-perfect cottage, for the weekend. The couple were larger than life and hugely entertaining. They were to remain friends for the next twenty or so years sharing with both Randolph and Serena the highs and lows of a roller-coaster life and all the eccentric moments in it.

A pair of donkeys brayed loudly in the neighbouring field as they kicked off with their first bottle of champagne. Serena noticed how luxurious the cottage was compared to her own. The cream carpet was sumptuous, the sofas low and plush. Antique furniture gleamed with beeswax polish. It made Serena think wistfully about all that she had lost. She wasn't often prone to these thoughts, but they crept in sometimes. Two small dogs demanded constant attention, and it became apparent to Serena that these were child substitutes. Liking her hosts and wishing to please them, she treated them with the attention the hosts expected for their 'babies'.

The following day, nursing a hangover, Randolph took her into the nearest market town where they visited an upmarket 'pre-loved' clothes shop. 'High time, you kitted yourself out in the correct fashion', he commented giving her figure a quick appraisal with his eyes. A tightly-fitting green velvet suit, an equally tight little black dress and a vibrant red checked jacket were purchased. In the shoe shop, which had a sale on, he bought her a pair of black crocodile court shoes and matching bag. She was so pleased and touched by the gifts that she failed to realise that she was being redesigned to his specifications and being groomed in more ways than one.

As the saying goes, there is none so blind as a fool in love. Serena had introduced Randolph to Luke with whom she maintained a cordial relationship for the sake of the children. 'What did you think of Randolph?' she had later asked him.

'Whatever gets you through the night' he had sneered, most uncharacteristically. Serena was horrified by his reaction; he was usually so easy-going. She had never known him make such an unkind remark before. She snorted with disbelief and convinced herself that he must be jealous that she had moved on. His own love life was in a state of flux at that point.

Luke's low opinion of Randolph became a bone of contention that eventually led to them being unable to communicate with each other. Serena would often wonder whether their friendship would have survived had it not been for Randolph's influence over her. The children might have had a father who would continue to provide both financial and emotional support, rather than ceasing all contact with them. After agonizing over this for many years, she eventually came to realise that she had unwittingly attracted weak men, and they, in turn, were attracted by her strength.

Randolph's Farm

The couple began to make the journey over to Randolph's farm more frequently as the days grew longer. The land that surrounded it was becoming neglected and overgrown. Sometimes they would both drive clapped-out, rusting tractors up and down the practically derelict fields whilst thick black smoke belched into the air. Serena had to twist a black plastic bag over the cracked seat of hers to protect herself from the grease that leaked everywhere and mysteriously appeared whenever she sat down. One week the wind was particularly unkind and cut straight through them both, as though summer was never going to arrive. She found herself balanced on the back of a planter and - as though in a daze - became hypnotised by the rhythm of the blade as it cut and penetrated through the rich soil.

They would sit huddled with their backs to the hedgerows where they would consume warm meat pies washed down with hot steaming tea laced with plenty of sugar. The raspberry canes and blackcurrants were beginning to produce quantities of soft fruit. Randolph claimed that the only way he could earn a living was through the harvest of the fruit on his land. He seemed to be at a loss for what else to do, as his debts escalated.

His old dog would faithfully shuffle up and down the rows of luscious green foliage as they picked the vibrant fruit, packed it all into boxes and stacked it in the car. Serena enjoyed the solitary nature of the work and the simple pleasure she took from working on the land. The days seemed to slip by with only occasional sightings of figures darting into the house, and they were mainly ignored and left alone. Serena found the lack of life in the house puzzling. No windows were ever opened and most of the curtains remained closed. It was as if the house swallowed up the family and held them prisoners. But they were also at war against the very person that had provided it all for them. Randolph would mutter darkly about a family curse which would follow him for the rest of his life. On the one occasion when his wife spoke to Serena, she was cordial enough before her feud with Randolph really kicked off, when Serena found herself used by Randolph as a buffer against both his bankers and his family. He was in a tight spot and desperate, and slowly but surely, he drew Serena into his web of deceit.

On Randolph's birthday and as was his custom he went on ahead to the house to set up the harvesting tools. They had secured a couple of Lithuanian men to assist with the work. They slept unseen under one of the large harvesters in the barn. When they ventured out, they crept stealthily between the rows of fruit with the family in the house oblivious to the work taking place on the land. Later in the season a coach load of over fifty fruit pickers would arrive at 5am and pick a field clean in just under two hours. No one in the house even stirred.

Serena had been busy baking a birthday cake which had taken an age to rise. As she drove over to the farm, she had a feeling of unease but couldn't identify it. The sight of a line of four-wheel drive cars greeted her, blocking the entrance to the yard. Men shifted uncomfortably in their tweed suit jackets and suspiciously shiny brogue shoes. Serena pulled up abruptly and was approached by a couple of burly men who turned out to be bailiffs. Farm machinery was being pulled out of the open barn and loaded onto a large trailer. Randolph was blazing with fury, and berating one of the suits, who hunched away from him, talking hurriedly into his phone.

A small group of interested onlookers had gathered from the village, the word having got around fast that Randolph was in trouble. They couldn't resist witnessing the spectacle and muttered snide comments, just loud enough to be heard.

'Finally got your come come-uppance, then' said one.

'How the mighty do fall' said another. Randolph was an outsider whom they had never understood or welcomed into their close-knit community. Turning to the mocking group and seeking out the main perpetrator of the petty comments, Randolph strode towards him. The man shrank back slightly as he realized he was in some danger of being punched then visibly relaxed as the scream of police sirens wailed up the drive. A stream of abuse poured forth from Randolph and rained over their heads.

Serena's car was now caught between the police and the huge trailer trying to remove the machinery. The police got out of their cars with weary resignation as excitement mounted in the huddled crowd. The scene was turning ugly. One of the bailiffs came within inches of Serena's face. 'At least I can pay my debts' he sneered. Never one to refuse a challenge, Serena was on her mettle.

'Do you have a name?' Serena asked, as she met his hard eyes with hers.

'No, and if I did, I wouldn't tell you' he replied.

'I know who you are' she said, 'you're a fat bastard who can only get his cheap thrills and bully people when you have the protection of authority behind you. You're nothing but scum of the earth, a common ugly fucker who gets off other people's pain and failure because you don't have the balls to attempt anything yourself'.

For a second, she thought he was going to hit her. One of the police stepped forward and laid a kindly restraining hand on her arm.

'Come on' he said gently, 'it's not worth it'.

She knew it wasn't, but her heart ached. She could hear the low hum of one of the farm tractors in the distance. Randolph must have left it running in one of the fields. There was no sign of the two Lithuanians, but she guessed they were hiding and watching the proceedings from afar. She hoped no-one else could hear it, because although old, it was very valuable. The rest of the farm machinery was now being loaded onto the large trailers with the police standing there to keep the peace. Randolph was speaking rapidly on his phone. 'Fuck it' he said looking at her despairingly, 'I'm going to lose the whole lot, the bitch has alerted the bailiffs on my birthday. She thought I wouldn't be here; how can anyone sink so low'?

But there had been good times. Serena would assist Randolph as he drove the tractor and would gently lay the green shoots of cane in the freshly turned soil. There was a gentle rhythm to the work as they went systematically up and down the rows, with a pleasing sense of motion and purpose. The hours would pass peacefully by whilst she shut out thoughts such as Luke's cold departure from their lives. She felt at home on the land and happy to be away from the confines of her four small walls. Each field had its own personality, its unique magic and special character. To be surrounded by tall raspberry canes at the height of the summer laden with luscious berries was magical. You could stand still and breathe in the heavy scent on the air or experience the thrill of parting back thick leaves to find another branch laden with ripe berries. You could be outside in the late autumn light and see the bushes turning, knowing that soon they would be bare and needing pruning in the harsh winter light.

You must love the land to experience this thrill. It was quite simply wasted on Randolph's wife who had never seemed to quite come to terms with leaving London. Luke was just like that too, a city boy at heart who floundered in the countryside. She would never forget sitting and driving a tractor in worn wellingtons and a frayed warm pullover and feeling the wind in her hair. She felt alive; it had been a mistake to marry a town boy.

Then Randolph was declared bankrupt, thanks to his dead brother Edward's lover. He would never understand, or come to terms with, why she had done this to him. He would visit his brother's grave and spit on it, cursing him for his duplicity. Yet Serena would later hear rumours that Randolph's ashes had been scattered there.

The family history was complicated and littered with the consequences of bitter quarrels. Edward had died young, blown up by a terrorist bomb, supposedly the victim of mistaken identity in a country rife with political unrest. It opened a can of worms, as instead of a mutual will that left Randolph with his brother's half of the farm business it had all been left to his girlfriend.

Edward had been a brilliant scholar. Dashing and good looking, he played the field with aplomb preferring parties and tennis to the tedium of running a farm. Bankrolled by their elderly father, resentment simmered between the brothers as Edward continued with his hedonistic bachelor lifestyle whilst Randolph was tied to a rapidly expanding young family

It was a terrible shock for Edward's grieving family when a woman stepped forward shortly after his burial, with a copy of a new will stating that Edward's fifty per cent of the business went entirely to her. And so it did, despite vigorous and expensive protestations to the courts. The elderly family solicitors who had not thought it their responsibility to inform the other two family members that the young man had secretly changed his will, took early retirement. The woman emptied Edward's home of his share of the family heirlooms as Randolph and his Father stood helplessly by and watched generations of family history disappear into a removal van.

'Surely she can't do this' the elderly man protested. But she could, and she did and there was nothing anyone could do to stop her. Because of the shock, Randolph's father died not long after Edward.

Randolph had bumped into the solicitors once at a cocktail party held for the counties finest. Their faces, ruddy with port, visibly paled as Randolph approached them. Their nervous wives twirled the stems of their elegant champagne glasses. Randolph stood and blocked their exit. 'May you rot in hell' he hissed and turned on his heels leaving them speechless. He never really recovered from Edward's betrayal, his mind constantly churning over all the possible reasons why he should have acted in this way. The process of losing so much poisoned his relationships with everyone around him and hardened his heart.

The End of the Fight

Randolph's childhood had been that of the privileged upper classes. He was the youngest of four children. Half- English, half-Russian, his mother was a White Russian émigré. She had written an unpublished autobiography, which Randolph always boasted he was going to edit and publish, claiming that it contained revelations that would rock the Establishment. He never did. He used to speak of the fabulous Fabergé eggs that the Tsarina had given his mother when she played at the palace with the young Russian royals, a favoured godchild of her's, by all accounts. No proof of this was ever forthcoming. No amount of furniture with stamps of the Tsar's Imperial palace or whispered tales of a certain bed, of which he was so proud, having belonged to one of the Princesses could mask the truth that he was in deep financial trouble.

The grandeur of his lineage meant nothing to the banks as they started to close in fast as his remaining funds dwindled. Serena begged him to record his childhood tales, the country house estates his Father would rent for the family, the lavish holidays they took, the homes they owned and many, often hilarious incidents. He wouldn't, instead preferring to pour another glass of wine and recount to a captive audience the ever-increasing stories of his past.

'One of my father's butlers on our Devon estate was called "Dad"' he would begin, 'damn confusing I can tell you, but rather unfortunate in that my own dear father ran the wretched fellow down as he lost control of his brand-new ride on lawn mower. Dear chap lost his leg' he added for extra effect. There was always a stunned silence after one of Randolph's party pieces.

They argued about this endlessly. 'Why don't you just *write it down*' Serena would implore him, 'it's such a fascinating story'. He would feign complete disinterest. 'It's the story of being related to royalty, inbred, dysfunctional, bastards born on the wrong side of the blanket' she would taunt. Nothing piqued his interest. He was blessed with a story which he threw away and discarded without so much as a backward glance. Rather like his families…

Bankrupts have no legal standing to fight through the courts so he wheedled and begged Serena to fight on his behalf. It never occurred to her that she would be put directly into the firing line. Such naivety, such stupidity, yet at the time she simply thought she was being loyal to her partner. Such a complete and utter waste of her precious time and resources. Serena went with Randolph and sat in the local solicitor's office to ask them to act for on his/her behalf. As if they could take on a major bank and win…but they charged a substantial amount in fees, wrote a couple of weak letters and got nowhere. Fighting a bank is only undertaken by people who are arrogant enough to believe they can win, with money they can afford to lose.

One of the senior partners had taken an instant dislike to Randolph and *vice versa*. Unfortunately, his children went to the same school as Sebastian and Scarlett. The nativity play that year was decidedly uncomfortable, as he took the opportunity to whisper what precisely he would do if his outstanding bills remained unpaid. Whilst adorable moppets clutching fluffy toy lambs acted out the Christmas story, Serena tried to ignore the scathing looks that were being directed at her. She thought at the time that this should have been a happy and touching occasion but as usual Randolph's neverending legal proceedings marred and overshadowed every aspect of their lives.

After parting with more money than Serena could bear to think about, they were directed to a firm of solicitors in the nearby city of Bristol. The senior partner of the firm had an impressive record of dealing with banks and situations just like Randolph's. Randolph explained that he had set up a limited company which might help to keep the house and the immediate curtilage safe from the threat of the banks. The inference was that the banks would have an impossible job issuing a repossession order on that, at least. The sale of the remaining land might well have appeased them.

This was just the first of many long meetings. An up and coming land agent had also been drafted in, a real hotshot, by all accounts; famed for unravelling the complexities of agricultural ties and limited companies − or more precisely − how to get around them. The team seemed excited by the prospect of outwitting the bank. 'Off the record' phone calls were made. The banks were quietly worried that Randolph had a very strong case.

But Serena was bored and frustrated. It wasn't her battle, she was sick of the acrimony directed at her and tired of the family's refusal to join forces. She was footing the bill after all, so she could afford to be pissed off by their attitude. Then the team turned towards her and explained their plan. All she had to do was buy the Trustee in bankruptcy's interest in the shares., and through her, Randolph could reclaim many of his more valuable goods and chattels.

Serena couldn't really think of a reason not to put her head above the parapet, the pool in which they all swam was small and they all knew each other so it was all very straightforward. All agreed that there were no risks to Serena or her home. Or rather that's what they implied. Randolph was so desperate he would show no mercy to anyone who deflected him from his purpose, including her, she realised. She agreed.

The battle that ensued between Randolph, his ex-wife and the banks was long, vicious and bloody. Having done her own deal with the creditors she couldn't play her part in saving the family home. If they had they all pulled together and closed ranks the outcome might well have been different.

The letters started to drop through Serena's letterbox without warning. There was one registered letter she would never forget. On thick embossed cream paper, it stated simply that unless she dropped her actions against the banks her home would be repossessed, and she would be made homeless. Clearly, she had been misled by Randolph. Was she just a pawn in a nasty game, an easy target? She was risking her children's home for a family she barely knew who couldn't tighten their belts when the going got tough. It seemed that untested theories and downright delusions were dished up before her daily.

Her father was singularly unimpressed. 'You're wasting your time and you could lose everything' he said irritably. Had other people played the game straightly from the start, something might have been salvaged. Serena managed to control her anger and swallow her bile, the futility and unpleasantness of it all choked her. Before the final day in court though, there were ugly scenes at the farm.

A group of travellers and gypsies, junkies and users of the worst kind appeared overnight and set up camp. Randolph could do nothing about it. They stuck needles up their arms in the day, dropped tabs, drank tins of strong lager and became abusive when it was suggested they work. Snotty nosed children curled up in dirty blankets sniffed miserably until the next tin of food was heated up. Forgotten cigarettes burned in overflowing ashtrays whilst used butts with tightly rolled up ends smouldered as the user forgot the latest joint as they sank into oblivion. Word had got around that the house was an easy target. It wasn't safe for anyone to be there alone and when twilight came Serena was relieved to be getting away from it all and back to her haven and home.

One day a small timid looking child approached her alarm etched all over her taut white face. 'My dad's ill' she said and tugged at Serena's sleeve imploringly. Serena approached the grubby looking caravan with some trepidation. The man was a drugs dealer with a reputation for violence, claiming to the police that he was entitled to be on the farmland as he was a seasonal worker. She pushed open the door and was repulsed by the sight that met her. Limp greying net curtains hung in a hopeless fashion at windows smeared with dirt. Battered saucepans sat piled high still encrusted with old food whilst a motionless figure lay hunched under an assorted pile of matted blankets.

The air was stifling with the stench of old cigarette smoke and cooking oil. A distinctive noise filled the air, unlike anything Serena had ever heard before. Coming from the hunched figure the sound of a grinding jaw and teeth scraping backwards and forwards over each other in a slow painful rhythm. Intermittent moans accompanied the sound. As the man turned slowly to face Serena, she was struck at how pitiful he looked. Gone was all the bravado and in its place, was a face bathed in beads of perspiration, sweat trickling down his stubby chin. 'I need painkillers' he gasped, 'it's my jaw you see'. He opened his mouth a fraction and Serena was horrified to see traces of yellow puss and poison amongst blackened loose teeth.

'You need a doctor' she replied 'and urgently. I'll phone one for you'. Afterwards he never stopped thanking her for saving his life. One day more and the poison would have seeped into his blood stream. He would probably have fallen unconscious and slipped away. Years later when she was walking through the local town, she was startled to hear her name being bellowed. Approaching her was a motley crew of assorted down and outs. Clutching tins of strong lager, holding onto thick leather dog leads with muscular panting dogs straining at the leash, they surrounded her. She felt acutely self-conscious of her smart clothes and cleanliness. Passers-by gave her curious stares and hurried on.

Before her was the man whose life she had saved, looking as ravaged as ever through drink and drug abuse. They all greeted her as though she were some long lost friend. He wrapped his arms round her, the distinctive smell of an unwashed body making her shudder with revulsion. When she eventually manged to untangle herself, she was aware of him singing her praises to his assorted friends. 'You coming for a beer?' he said suddenly. She declined and hastily made excuses to move on. She reflected on the fine line between addiction and recreational drug use, recalling the small girl's terror and helplessness. Had this dealer simply died others may have been saved. She would never know.

Randolph's fight all ended abruptly one day in the high courts. The big guns were there representing the banks, clutching onto their fat briefcases and laughing confidently. Randolph was told to sit quietly and for once he did so. The might of the opposition's legal team shot any other arguments down in flames. Randolph had no representation. He had run out of money and had to stand his legal team down, much to their chagrin. They always maintained that they'd come close to giving the banks a run for their money.

Serena fervently wished she had turned her back on them all, stepped down and walked away. It would have all been so much simpler.

Old Friends

Randolph took Serena to visit some old shooting friends of his parents. They drove down a long winding muddy drive and were confronted by a house that looked as though it had landed there from a bygone era. They were warmly welcomed by a sturdily-built woman with terribly clipped vowels who led them into the kitchen and gestured towards a high-backed wooden settle. The table was laid with bone china and polished silver on a worn but starched linen cloth. A decanter held the claret which would accompany the lunch – game, of course. The delicious aroma of pheasant casserole permeated the air, but there was absolutely no chance of the wine warming up.

Serena had never been in such a chilly and stark kitchen, although it was rather beautiful in its own way. Through the leaded windows, she could see pheasants strutting and pecking for seeds in the garden. An electric fire glowed by their feet but really made little or no difference to the temperature of the room. The hostess rubbed her gnarled fingers together and wrapped one of her layers more firmly around her substantial frame. Her Harris tweed skirt and thick woollen stockings protected her from the cold. She looked at Serena inquisitively but politely.

The door burst open and a ruddy faced man leered towards her. 'Who in god's name is this beauty?' he enquired. He had obviously already started on his lunchtime aperitif before they arrived. Above his head hung a sturdy clear plastic bag hanging on string with a large colourful plastic fish inside. It was entirely out of keeping with the rest of the room, but Serena was fascinated. The claret began to flow, mellowing the spartan atmosphere. It transpired that their host had suffered from an acrimonious divorce and had been disowned by his entire family. His second wife was younger, and his full-time carer.

He wore a stout pair of corduroy trousers and a well-worn pullover covered in bobbles and left-over food. Thick nasal and ear hair had been allowed to grow unchecked, giving him a wild and unkempt air. Eating, drinking and reminiscing about his past were his only pleasures these days. Serena asked politely if she could use the lavatory. She had once inadvertently used the word 'toilet' and been severely reprimanded by Randolph. If only she had gone the full hog and said serviette instead of napkin, patio rather than terrace, held her knife like a pencil and spoken in a thick regional accent she would have succeeded in repulsing him... She was led past rows and rows of worn country coats, wellingtons, walking boots, dog leads, chipped flower pots, fossils galore and heaps of sticks and driftwood in the freezing cold passageway to the bathroom. There was a tap dripping slowly above a worn pale green plastic bucket in the cracked china sink. Crockery was piled up inside. 'This is where I wash the dishes' her hostess explained.

Serena entered a bleak bathroom, slightly warmed by a single bar electric heater. Thin patterned towels, still slightly damp, were draped over a white bath tub which sported a large brown stain. A white plastic line supported a tired looking curtain from which the last rays of weak winter sunshine filtered through. Serena lowered herself onto the black loo seat gingerly. Fortunately, she had not consumed enough of the robust red wine to risk falling off the seat, as the icy cold plastic met her warm backside. Afterwards she turned on the taps cautiously and was startled by the rush of murky brown water as she washed her hands with the remains of the soggy Wright's cold tar soap. She thought of the people she knew who wallowed in unashamed luxury. The cheerless room disturbed her, and yet they both looked hearty and healthy. Happiness and contentment come from within and not from material possessions, she reminded herself.

By the time she returned to the table, a bottle of port had been produced from the cellar. There was a lot of discussion about its age, origins and merits. The host raised a glass.

'Here's to this marvellous young woman who has saved this fine gentleman's life'.

It hadn't occurred to Serena that she had rescued Randolph, and she didn't think that she had. Only many years later would she realise the truth of this statement. When you are the rock that people cling to, you are simply unaware of your strength until there is a need to save yourself. If unlucky, you find that time after time you must be your own rescuer.

Their host leant forward in a rather conspiratorial way, as though to impart some important advice. He must have had a twinkle in his eye at some state in his life, but it had faded from years of alcohol abuse and the stress of family rifts.

'I always say to chaps embarking on a new venture with a lady friend of one important thing' he said, pausing to refresh his glass. 'Always pick one with less money than yourself, that way they can't accuse you of being a kept man'. Considering Randolph was seriously on his uppers, his comment made Serena bristle with indignation. 'The stupid old goat' she thought. The bottle was finished. 'More wine, woman' he bellowed as he unsuccessfully tried to remove himself from the seat where his substantial backside was embedded.

As they left, they had jars of home-made jam and preserves pushed into their hands, the labels scrawled with spidery blue biro.

Serena reflected that despite their reduced circumstances, they obviously adored each other. Maybe it was possible for her and Randolph to achieve a similar equilibrium.

Scotland Beckons

Every year Randolph would go to stay with a friend on his blackcurrant farm in Scotland and help with the harvesting. He had supposedly designed a blackcurrant harvester but had omitted to patent the design, which led to it being successfully copied. For him, it was a busman's holiday and he would be driving up, but he suggested that Serena join him later, and she happily agreed. It was a while since she had been on an extended trip away from the confines of the village and it sounded rather adventurous taking a long journey on the train alone.

'Before I go, I have to look for a co-driver for the harvester' explained Randolph. 'I always go for young girls, they work so much harder'. Serena must have looked perplexed, so he continued. 'They don't drive off the rows of bushes, looking at female backsides as they bend over unlike young chaps' he said.

Who in god's name was he kidding? Seeing her expression, he said hastily 'Come and meet the girl I've picked' he suggested 'and we'll go to the pub'. Sitting in the garden of the pub, Serena thought wistfully back to all happy times she had shared with the children in that very spot. A milk float had once been parked there, keeping them entertained for hours as they all clambered on and off, engrossed in their make-believe world.

A girl arrived clutching a pint of cider and Randolph introduced her. She seemed nice enough but struck Serena as rather plain and dumpy. Randolph kept the drinks flowing as only he knew how. As he disappeared to the bar again, the two women were left alone. 'You mustn't mind that he came and stayed with me' the girl informed her. 'nothing happened between us, he slept on the floor'.

Serena's face must have registered her enormous surprise. Here she was faced with a young, rather nondescript girl who was about to be employed by her live-in lover, spending a lot of time alone with him and now she had innocently let slip that he had stayed the night in her flat. He had, once again omitted to tell Serena the full story. She was infuriated by his deceit but when she confronted him later, he slid off the hook with ease by telling her she was over-reacting. 'As usual'.

Overcoming her misgivings, Serena went ahead and took the train up to Scotland. She hadn't been before and found the contrasting colours of the landscape exhilarating. They seemed to drive for miles and miles after Randolph had picked her up at the station, passing through villages consisting of dark stone buildings clustered around a solitary high street.

'The off licence and chippie' Randolph announced when they arrived at their destination, 'the mainstays of our village'. They continued and turned up a long dirt track eventually pulling up at a house surrounded by lots of large metal outbuildings, seemingly put up at random. An assortment of dogs all shapes and sizes greeted them, barking furiously as they circled around the car. At the back of the house a bright red door stood ajar.

'Come in and meet everyone' Randolph said. They walked through a cluttered cloakroom, the floor piled high with discarded clothes and into a kitchen in equal disarray. The table in the middle was cluttered with papers. An elderly man in a flat cap was introduced as 'Papa, the head of the clan'. His brown leather belt held up his trousers. 'We'll all be needing a cup of tea' he announced and sat down wearily.

A younger couple appeared and were introduced as Morag and Alastair. Serena's first impression was of a happy, laid-back couple. They were hardworking, honest and straightforward without any hidden agenda. Alastair was wiry with a ginger beard speckled with grey. His face was covered in sandy coloured freckles as were the backs of his hands. When he spoke, it was with a thick Scottish regional accent. Morag wore a long denim skirt and sported bright pink lipstick and a wide friendly smile. 'You'll be Serena then' she said, 'we've heard lots about you'. Her cheeks glowed with rude health and outdoor living. 'I guess you'll want to see where we are staying' Randolph eventually said.

Serena had observed on their way in that the farm was surrounded by faded blue, green and cream coloured caravans in which she presumed the pickers and their families were staying. She learnt that these people returned year after year, treating the break as their annual holiday. They were bussed in from the city courtesy of Alastair. Corrugated iron buildings housed families who had been coming for generations, further back than even Papa could recall. This accommodation was fiercely guarded and fought for as it was viewed as superior. Serena began to wonder where they were staying, the farmhouse maybe? 'Back in the car then' Randolph ordered. They crawled slowly down one of the dirt tracks passing families sitting outside in large groups idling the rest of the afternoon away after an early morning start. They pulled up outside a dirty caravan.

Randolph had to be joking, surely. Serena had never stepped inside such a place, never mind slept in one. They stepped out of the car and he went forward and opened the flimsy door. There was a faint shriek from within the musty smelling interior. Standing only in her bra and knickers was Randolph's co-driver, looking even more dumpy and plain than Serena remembered.

'You could have knocked first' she grumbled yet she seemed strangely unconcerned by her semi-nudity. Randolph seemed equally unconcerned, no doubt he had viewed it all before, perhaps more, who could tell? On the stained patterned carpet more greying underwear was strewn. Off the seating area was a room with a double bed to which there was no door, privacy was obviously not an option. 'Here we are then' announced Randolph indicating the space in an unconcerned fashion.

It took Serena a while to assess the situation. She had one of two choices; stay or go. She could hardly believe that she was expected to sleep in this cramped area with a young girl scarcely a foot away from them. She should have refused there and then. His ex-wife would not have tolerated it nor would any of his fancy married lovers. On the other hand they were all pretty high-maintenance. Randolph had frequently complimented her on her willingness to get her hands dirty, and muck in. 'We make a good team' he had said, warming her heart. She would just have to put up and shut up. She sensed that the girl was taken aback by the timing of her arrival; no doubt Randolph had sprung it on her. Ignoring the tension, Randolph opened a bottle of wine, his usual answer to any awkward situation was to get drunk. Serena and the girl matched him drink for drink, uniting in deriding the caravan of his choice and giggling together. He threw them withering looks and resorted to saying that they were rude and vulgar hoydens. Initially, Randolph seemed uneasy, probably with good reason Serena thought, but eventually became less sour faced after several large glasses of whisky. But she was still angry inside. Was this smelly caravan really his idea of a treat for her? She thought about the hints he had dropped about his previous liaisons, conducted in grand hotels and picturesque locations. Only the restorative effect of the wine prevented her from stomping off.

The girl, whose name Serena genuinely had forgotten, took her on a tour of the fruit farm. It was pretty grim, to Serena's mind. The people looked rough and uncouth. They were from tough estates in Glasgow and when they spoke, she barely understood a word they said though she could make out the swear words clearly enough. They nodded to her as she passed them. She could have been from planet Mars, she felt so different. 'You'll be the toff's missis then' one remarked. The girl led her into a dark concrete building, best described as a brick shit house which is precisely what it was.

Rows of lavatories with huge gaps under the doors and sodden loo paper trampled underfoot confronted her. It was that awful hard, shiny loo paper too; the very worst to her mind. The porcelain sinks each lay full of grey soapy water whilst women rubbed hard at worn clothing. 'This is where we wash' the girl explained. 'Really?' said Serena faintly. The girl gave her a pitying look. 'The showers are even shittier' she said, 'people barge in on you, they get pissed off with waiting, see'. Serena saw only too clearly.

The next morning, armed with their towels they made the miserable walk to the cold damp washhouse. But Serena experienced the torture of stripping off to wash on this first day. On hearing she had done this Morag immediately offered her the use of the farm shower. 'Randolph wouldn't dream of washing alongside the others' she said. 'Why the hell hadn't he said so?' Serena muttered to herself. And she had shared the caravan with the girl on the first night, before she made it abundantly clear she wasn't happy with the arrangement. Randolph shot her an amused look. 'I'll see what I can arrange' he promised. Shortly afterwards Alastair arrived and knocked politely. Sticking his head round the door, he surveyed the cramped scene. 'You'll be needing yourselves a bit of privacy, then' he observed, and led them to another dubious van.

It was fun in the end, life and situations are what you make of them, and for several years afterwards she took the children up with her. They would arrive and head for the nearest charity shop where she would kit them out with all the clothes they would need for the two weeks harvesting. They would be worn day in, day out and get filthy with blackcurrant juice, dirt and squashed berries. On the last day they would be placed in a black bin bag and discarded. That evening they would all dress up and go somewhere grand for dinner. The pickers would get uproariously drunk and swapping partners and loose sexual encounters were commonplace. One year on their return from the final night the children were amazed to see a man so drunk he could hardly stand parading around in women's underwear. Quite an education really.

Serena maintained that a preservation order should have been placed on the entire site. It was a way of life that would be lost as machines replaced people. She later learnt that in his final days Randolph had helped Alastair and Morag renovate some of the old wooden huts and one of them bore a plaque in his memory.

She wondered if he had ever remembered them all sitting up high on top of the machine as it made its way slowly up and down the rows of blackcurrants. They would equip themselves with packets of sweets and be lulled into a stupor by the rhythmic throbbing of the thrashers as they cut through and opened the bushes, shaking the branches as the berries tumbled into the tray. On the back of the harvester the men rode on a back plate hauling the heavy crates of black sticky fruit one on top of another until the end of the row where the tractor would come and ease the trays gently off. In this short space of time the men would roll themselves a quick fag and pop it between their rotten teeth. A man called Walter who was booze addled and wizened by years of smoking would gently clip Sebastian round the ear. 'Why can't you help us, you lazy little fucker' he spat out. Serena was mortified at first. 'He's only nine years old' she said, quickly springing to his defence. But Sebastian looked thrilled at the idea of mucking in and quickly clambered down from the top of the machine and onto the platform with them. They jostled together and welcomed him aboard.

He looked so tiny and vulnerable amongst these strangers but gallantly started trying to assist. He loved it and they respected the little boy from a prep school, getting his hands dirty too. He never once complained of being tired and worked alongside them to the best of his ability. Whether he could understand a word of their thick accents Serena couldn't tell but there was an awful lot of laughter and good-nature teasing. As the days went by, he became more and more stained with the startling colour of the berries, his pale face becoming healthily tanned. At the end they had a whip round for him. He had never had such a large amount of money in his little hands, his eyes opened wide in surprise.

'You're a good lad' they said and, so he was. Serena was proud of him with good reason. It would be nice to think that Randolph had spared her son a thought.

Suffolk

Serena decided she needed to get away from it all so went with the children to a well-known author's house deep in the Suffolk countryside which her friend Bella was house sitting.

Randolph announced that he too needed to get away and magically conjured up the funds to join some old friends on an exotic island, flying via New York first. They would not see each other for three weeks, and frankly Serena was glad to have a break from his personal baggage. She waved cheerily, as he set off from the cottage. Rolling down the window, he declared his undying love for her.

But he didn't go to the airport straight away as he told her he would. She found out later that he had stopped off for the night at an old friend's and enjoyed a day at the races with a party of glamorous women. She would later find photographs of him in a dapper suit and one of his Hermes ties, whilst a woman in a large black hat with elegantly crossed ankles smiled winsomely into the camera. Serena was livid when these pictures came to light.

'Why do you feel the need to lie to me?' she demanded.

'Because I know you would only kick up a fuss, and I was right" he snapped. 'Anyway, it was only a white lie'. Randolph had so many excuses for his avoidance of the truth.

The author's house was gorgeous, and Serena soon pushed Randolph to the back of her mind. It was everything that a Suffolk farmhouse should be. It was a rare treat for the children to have any kind of holiday, and they adored it. In the grounds around the farm there was an old gypsy caravan which the children spent hours in. Chickens roamed and pecked happily round the garden beds whilst behind electric fencing were a huge black potbellied pig and several Suffolk Punch horses. A gentle lurcher allowed Sebastian and Scarlett to pet and hug her.

They took trips to Southwold and Walberswick, and the children ran shrieking into the cold North Sea.

Bella's boyfriend, a prominent journalist on a left-wing newspaper joined them too. When, in a phone call, Randolph found out who they were holidaying with, he was blisteringly scornful and ran the paper down, chuntering about what he would say to the journalist should he ever meet him.

'You never will' said Serena crossly, 'Carry on getting blind drunk with your cronies'. She didn't want him spoiling the pleasure she was taking in this break. She felt so relaxed. A comfortable pair of red plush velvet sofas sat in a drawing room lined with bookshelves crammed to the gill. When the children were asleep, Serena and Bella sat and read books and perused glossy magazines whilst languidly swinging their legs off the ends.

The kitchen was everything Serena had ever dreamt of and secretly craved. She loved the four-door blue Aga which Londoner Bella was slightly afraid of. They all ate supper at the scrubbed pine table in the centre of the room, cooking together amicably. The house was easy to live in, but it did belong to a highly successful media couple and a fax machine squatted next to the bread bin. It endlessly churned out messages which Bella diligently put in their in-trays.

It wasn't long before Randolph started sending Serena faxes and she returned them with quaint cartoon scribblings reflecting their relationship. They featured a spindly man with knobbly knees and a woman in high heels and a tight, short skirt.

'They're awfully sweet,' Bella remarked, 'but somehow, also a bit sinister'. She was obliquely referring to her suspicion that Randolph was developing an unhealthy hold over her friend. Maybe it was a premonition.

The Proposal

Alastair and Morag arrived from Scotland for what Randolph called a 'jolly'. A jolly involved long drawn-out lunches with copious amounts of wine. They decided they would go to Burton Bradstock, a well-known spot on the coast with a wonderful seafood restaurant. The weather was mild for October and in an azure sky, seagulls screeched above them as they dived for scraps of food.

Everyone was in high spirits. As usual, Randolph ordered oysters. They relished the distinctive salty taste, the unmistakable feel as the delicacy slipped down their throats. Next, they ate crab claws, carefully picking out and savouring the flesh. Two empty bottles of white wine were removed, and their successor lay nestling in a frosted ice bucket as they succumbed thoroughly to the pleasure of the moment.

During lunch, the sea had a gentle swell with only small white horses breaking the surface. But as they finished their meal, the waves started to break at the point where the sand shelved deeply. Randolph wanted to swim, and should have noticed the danger signs, but refused to listen when Serena asked him not to, particularly after drinking.

She tutted. It was pure madness and hubris, and as he jauntily made his way down to the sea in his baggy swimming trunks, Serena was uneasily aware that everyone else was exiting the water. The sea was cold, but it was completely in character for Randolph to swagger on. He loved to *épater les bourgeois;* to cause people to stare and gasp in horror. Swimming easily in the shallows, he made for deeper water. But within minutes the waves were crashing and rolling alarmingly. Serena looked out from the restaurant's terrace to see him making his way further out to avoid the swell. It was obvious he could not exit the water now; the waves had become frighteningly powerful. She began to feel panicky.

The three of them looked worriedly at each other. 'He'll be okay, I'm sure' Alastair said, failing to keep the uncertainty from his voice.

The situation swiftly got out of hand. Pushing back her chair with a clatter, Serena ran towards the water's edge. The waves were swollen and menacing as each one hurtled towards the shore. She could make out Randolph as he appeared bobbing between them, but it was impossible for him to get to the safety of the shore. He tried a couple of times but was unsuccessful. Each time he attempted to come closer the power of the sea pulled him right back.

It was as if Poseidon himself was playing with Randolph, punishing him for his arrogance. The waves were now crashing fearfully onto the ledge, the tide was turning, and it was a death trap. Knuckles pressed to her mouth in horror, Serena knew that in a split second it could go either way. The undercurrent sucked noisily and greedily over the thousands of pebbles, which clashed martially as they collided against each other.

Suddenly there he was, a tiny powerless dot in her sight line. She couldn't get any closer or she would be sucked under herself. But behind him, she could see the terrifying height of a large wave on the verge of breaking. He stared directly at her, his face etched with fear, his eyes speaking to her imploringly.

'I'm going to drown' they said, and as if reading his thoughts, the sea took him and tossed him like a piece of flotsam. Down he went, sucked right under. Serena held her breath. Someone further up the beach was running for the life-belt, people were gathering at the shoreline in concerned clusters, straining to see what was happening.

After what felt like a lifetime, Randolph reappeared, and Serena exhaled thankfully. But, she calculated, he was rapidly running out of time, and must be too weak to stand up. She had never seen anyone dying in front of her. What would life be like without him? She was merely a few feet away from him, the spume frothing at her feet. She knew then that she loved him and would grieve for him, though even then the thought crossed her mind that she was feeling a mix of fear and compassion.

As she watched, his body shuddered as it fought to reach safety. Somewhere in the distance a woman was screaming as the lifebelt was hurled in his direction, but the angry ocean spat it back and it missed his outstretched arms. Then all at once, another wave swiftly propelled him forward and regurgitated him onto the pebbles at her feet. He lay looking up at her.

'Hello, you' he said gasping for breath, 'I think we should get married'.

It was as though nothing untoward had happened.

And that was that. 'Eat, drink and be merry, or tomorrow we may die', and we might as well tie the knot too, Serena thought, her tired brain resorting to cliché. The celebrations started immediately with two fine bottles of red. Four of the juiciest, thickest steaks were purchased from the local butcher. On hearing of Randolph's close shave, he admitted to being caught out at the very same spot.

'Quite a few have been lost out there' he informed them, gravely. Serena shivered.

The foursome trooped back to the house which Randolph and Serena had recently moved to. He had persuaded her to sell her cottage, as he felt it was just too small for their needs. They were renting from the owners of a shooting estate and Serena wasn't happy about this. The building looked quirky enough from the outside, but she had, as usual, had to work hard to make it look comfortable and inviting within the limits of their tenancy agreement.

As she toasted her own engagement, she silently prayed that her married life would involve owning her own home again.

Wedding Bells Ring

Randolph and Serena were married on a frosty late December afternoon, an intimate gathering in the small church on the Estate, followed by a reception in the village hall.

It wasn't the stress-free occasion it should have been. Their caterer Sian had let them down at the last minute. The couple had been scaping a living by growing soft fruits in poly tunnels on rented farmland. The initial investment had further eroded the proceeds of the sale of Serena's cottage. Just a week before the wedding, an almighty storm had wrecked the tunnels and exposed their tender plants. The farm landlords had got down on their hands and knees, trying to salvage the crop. But Sian was coldly unsympathetic, fearing they would be unable to pay her bill after this disaster.

Serena was therefore late for her own wedding as she had been forced to cook an enormous pot of *boeuf bourguignon*. It was bubbling away on her ancient stove, perilously close to her wedding finery. Giving it a final stir, she removed her apron, and hastily checked her appearance in an ancient mirror. Her father had bought her a long, deep red velvet dress with a jewelled collar. It was lined with vivid pink silk, and she felt momentarily cheered by its beauty.

Walking down the long drive from the house to the church she strove to feel serene and composed. Her thoughts seemed loud in the silent twilight. Wisps of woodsmoke from the houses she passed lingered on the air. A sparkling frost began to settle on the thin branches of the naked trees that lined the walk.

Friends had travelled up from London and encouraged by Randolph (of course) had taken over the local pub. They were now huddled in the cold church, breathing out fumes of alcohol. The party had begun without her, she thought, as she took her father's arm and processed towards Randolph, stepping carefully on the uneven flagstones. It was considered a privilege to be married in this quaintly unique manorial church.

The wedding service passed by in a blur. Serena would later wonder how many brides before her would look back and rue the day they ever vowed 'to love and to cherish, in sickness and in health, for richer or poorer, till death do us part' She hadn't promised to obey; a small act of rebellion.

At the end of the service, the Lord of the Manor, in fraying plus fours, leapt forward to the thick cord of the church bell and pulled on it with all his might. It was a charming gesture. The clear sound pierced the night air as they left the church to smiles and congratulations. The path to the village hall was illuminated by burning candles. The indigo blue of the sky was scattered with the first of the evening stars. The happy chattering crowd were revelling in attending such an offbeat wedding.

The village hall was more used to shooting parties than wedding receptions. Above a roaring log fire were mounted ancient stags' heads which Serena's mother Evelyn had festooned with trailing ivy and holly, thick with glistening berries. Each table was draped with beautiful damask table cloths.   A host of candles lit the room, their golden light cleverly disguising the hall's functional shape. Randolph's family silver gleamed here and there amongst the abundant flowers and foliage which Evelyn had fashioned into exquisite arrangements.

The love, creativity and enthusiasm of family and friends had worked its magic that night, and the room would not, Serena reflected, look out of place in *House and Garden*. Her spirits rose, as the increasingly lively guests vied for space against the large Christmas tree twinkling in the corner. Scarlett, and Georgina's daughter Cressida were the tiny bridesmaids, happy and excited in their berry-red frocks. When the music started, they twirled and swirled together on the floor.

Sebastian stepped forward, his face alive with delight and announced that he was terribly happy they had got married. He was now thirteen. On this night, Serena could not have imagined what lay ahead; the incessant bullying Randolph would inflict on this child as he grew up. The party roared on and Serena ceased to feel any misgivings. Here and now, despite their recent setback, with every glass of champagne poured, the future seemed full of promise.

But from that day forth, her life ceased to be her own.

Because their crop had been ruined, they couldn't afford a honeymoon. The business was no longer sustainable. They were forced to cut their losses and think about the future. They pondered the way forward, drinking cheap red wine and buying only marked down items from the local supermarket

However, Randolph had finally secured some family heirlooms after years of bickering. His family were unaware that he was going to sell these, nor that he owed this chance to Serena, who had paid a cash amount to the Trustee in Bankruptcy to arrange this. Randolph began to dwell on his past.

Mysterious Past

Randolph was to be interviewed for a local paper after the news leaked out that he was selling some valuable items. This greatly appealed to his vanity and he began to see himself as some sort of celebrity. When the journalist arrived, Randolph ordered Serena to leave them alone, and positioned himself in front of a merry crackling fire, a small sherry in a cut glass at his side. The following is based on a small extract of the story as it was reported.

"The complex and compelling life of a beautiful Russian émigré is slowly shedding its mystery. The Russian orphan, god-daughter to the murdered Tsarina Alexandra, led a colourful existence, escaping from the horror of the 1917 revolution before being caught up in the East-West spying game and finally settling to married life in Britain".

(At this point it explained that her story and her identity were about to be revealed in her autobiography edited by Randolph…)

The piece continued:

"One of the gifts the Tsarina gave her god-daughter was a necklace made of miniature Fabergé eggs which she passed down to Randolph. Items which he considers too precious to dispose of include the bed slept in by the Tsarina's murdered sister Princess Ella and a large imposing mirror which once stood in an Imperial palace"

This just made Serena sigh. They had once been at a party when Randolph learnt that their hostess was related to a senior KGB agent some generations previously. Randolph curtly informed her that his mother had actually helped to trap her relation, whose activities were nothing to be proud of.

'Your family has blood on their hands' he declared, so naturally they were immediately asked to leave. Such was life with Randolph.

The auction of the selected items eventually took place and a not insignificant sum was raised. Randolph was buoyed up by the sight of his remaining effects, possibly thinking that by surrounding himself with them he would once again have the entrée into 'society'. He paid for embossed invitations to a Sunday morning sherry party. Everyone whom he considered worthy of notice was invited to come and admire his artefacts. They came, stared and clearly wondered how this mismatched pair, living in a scruffy rented house, came to be surrounded by fine family portraits, exquisite Persian rugs, miniatures in gold frames, and silver *objects d' art* displayed in a fine cabinet. Randolph was in his element and unbearably smug when his story appeared in the paper.

However, because of the auction there was finally money in the bank, providing a small degree of security. Serena managed to sell off what remained of the fruit business to a local man who was keen to try his hand at growing organic produce. She never recovered her investment, something Randolph would conveniently forget as he forged ahead with yet another business proposition. But she was saddened by the demise of the poly tunnel project. They had spent nights on site in a dilapidated vintage caravan. It was lined with wooden panelling, yellow with the previous owner's nicotine, and featured a glass-fronted drinks cabinet. Serena had taken photographs of them all grinning inside this absurdly wacky space as they lived like gypsies for a few nights. It had been fun. But now Randolph was ready to start again.

Edwina and Luke

Though not entirely oblivious to the adult world, the children were happily attending local schools. Sebastian was at a top grammar whilst Scarlett was secure at a small prep school nearby. That they were potential Oxbridge candidates had been mentioned by both their respective teachers and Serena felt inordinately proud of them.

But money matters constantly invaded her thoughts. Previously Serena had barely been able to afford the school uniforms. Music lessons, horse riding, or school trips abroad were simply out of the question. Scarlett's school fees were still being paid through a trust fund set up by Luke's father, who had recently died. Luke's visits to his children were becoming more infrequent and his hostility to Serena had increased. He had found himself a wealthy new girlfriend, whom he would go on to marry. Now he and his mother Edwina became potential creditors.

When Luke had abandoned his small family, Edwina offered to repay the original deposit on the cottage rather than see Serena struggle. Serena had accepted, feeling that it was the least she could do, since her son was so fiscally incompetent. But since her marriage to Randolph, Edwina was threatening to sue her for the paltry profit she had made from the sale of the cottage. Though Serena protested that Luke had lost them their original family home, Edwina went ahead and took her to court.

Fortunately, the judge dismissed the case swiftly, telling Luke and his mother in no uncertain terms that there was nothing to be repaid and nothing to be divided, as the small deposit his mother had put down was the least this wealthy family could do for their own flesh and blood. It wasn't as though Edwina had any other grandchildren. She had even had the gall to suggest that Serena should apply for a council flat.

Luke was a bad loser. Serena guessed that he and his mother both loathed Randolph and were trying to exert what little power over her they still possessed. Yet she had often felt that Luke treated her as an unpaid nanny rather than the mother of his children.

Some years later, hearing that Edwina was seriously ill, Serena put her own resentment aside and took both children to see their grandmother. Weakened and bed-ridden, what she told Serena was upsetting and alarming. It seemed that all the animosity had emanated from Luke. Overjoyed to see Sebastian and Scarlett, Edwina took Serena's hand between her own thin one, and whispered:

'I never wanted to involve you in court proceedings at all' she confessed. 'But Luke told me you didn't want to see me, didn't even want me to have your address to send the children a birthday present. I was hurt'.

'Not a day went by when I didn't think of them' she said continued sadly, turning to Serena for an explanation. Serena was appalled by her words, but before she could reply, Luke himself unexpectedly appeared, suspicious of Serena's motives. She swallowed her anger. She would not challenge him and distress Sebastian and Scarlett who hadn't seen him for far too long. Yet she struggled to comprehend how anyone could tell such a cruel lie to his own mother. Luke's emotions could be turned on and off at will, it transpired.

In future, Serena would write begging letters to him pleading with him to contact the children, but he refused, telling her they were now her sole responsibility. Randolph would shout at her to chase him for maintenance money, but Luke slyly slipped through the net by claiming he was unemployed and had no income.

When Edwina eventually died, Luke didn't bother to inform Serena; Evelyn read about it in *The Telegraph*. Luke must have removed the contact number that Serena had left on Edwina's fridge so that no one else could find her. A diamond necklace that Edwina had promised to leave to Scarlett, her only granddaughter, went instead to Luke's second wife. He had invoked a power of attorney on grounds of her mild dementia and simply informed her that she had bequeathed it elsewhere.

On the morning of the funeral Serena allowed the children to take the day off school so they could observe the passing of their grandmother. They had walked along deserted country lanes with the sun high above them in a clear blue sky. She could hear a skylark in the distance and noticed the wild flowers beginning to appear on the banks.

'Didn't Grandma London love us?' asked Scarlett. The question was direct and hovered on the air waiting for a satisfactory answer.

'Very much' Serena answered, 'She told me how often she thought about you when we saw her last time'. Then Sebastian asked the question she dreaded most.

'What about Daddy?' he said plaintively. 'Does daddy not love us anymore?'. Serena's heart pounded in her chest. How could she answer? They were getting too old now to be fobbed off with the white lies she had previously told them, to protect their feelings.

'Let's concentrate on happier times' she suggested.

In fact, they would never see their father again. He had known as he waved them off from his mother's flat, with a beaming smile and false promises to keep in touch, that after his mother's death he would take his considerable inheritance, move abroad and begin a new family. Sebastian and Scarlett were effectively wiped out of his life. Though Serena would always tell them that this cruel rejection was not their fault, and that they must not dwell on it, her sorrow for their pain never left her. She would forever suspect that she herself had let them down, by picking a weak, second-rate man to father her children.

As Edwina had quietly said to her about her only son 'I love him, but he disappoints me'.

We're Going to France...

Randolph suddenly announced that they were moving to France. The damp house on the estate bored him and so off he set on a fact-finding mission to the south of France, leaving Serena behind in the cold and the mud. He justified this by insisting that it was term-time, and she had the children and his ailing dog to look after.

He could scarcely hide his glee as he packed his suitcase and waved goodbye. They had just taken delivery of a home computer, more of a rarity then. It couldn't have had a Firewall on it, since the most hideous messages kept flashing up at her in his absence.

' I know you are there' one read, 'you can't hide'. Could it really be intended for her? She was suspicious, and with good reason. During his trip to France, a mysterious contact of Randolph's offered him a part-time contract as a kidnap negotiator, which would involve periodic travel to some of the more dangerous countries in Latin America. He phoned to relay this news, playing down the risks.

The salary offered meant that they could have stayed in England, but he was hell bent on getting away. ' I have to have the channel between us' he kept repeating whenever she worried about this life-changing move. By 'us' he was referring to his estranged family. They wrongly believed that Randolph was hiding a fortune through an offshore trust that he had once owned. It had long been emptied. Randolph had used the dregs of it to take one of his daughters on a smart holiday, in a futile attempt at reconciliation before he was declared bankrupt.

Now Randolph was prepared to move away from his family without a backward glance. 'When I turn my back on you, you cease to exist' was his mantra, and many more people were to discover the truth of this.

Meanwhile their daily routine trundled on, two school runs, early starts on winter mornings, deep mud tracks from the drive to the front door, shoes hastily wiped on a sodden doormat and a leaking roof to a car that was only fit to ride in if you placed a plastic bag on the seat. Accusations that they lived high on hog made Serena smile ruefully. Every last penny was accounted for.

Randolph eventually returned from his French jaunt with lots of coloured pictures depicting enticing looking houses with equally enticing low prices. Ancient stone buildings garlanded with ivy and bougainvillea nestled prettily between vineyards and sunflowers., simply oozing Gallic charm. He waited until Serena had looked her fill and then baldly announced that

'I've bought a house'.

Enjoying the look of shock on her face, he continued 'We'll move in two months'. The harsh reality was that Randolph needed the English Channel between himself and his ex-wife. He fantasised constantly about murdering her, bemoaning the fact he hadn't already done so.

'I would have done my time by now' he would slur after a bout of drinking. He recounted lurid tales which shocked Serena and which she would never repeat. They were a tissue of lies spun round a central web of deceit. Serena had hoped she might change him, but any woman who thinks she can alter a man who has led a double life for years and is skilled at twisting the truth is only fooling herself. He was vague about the number of affairs he had conducted, though he wasn't above dropping a few titled names when he felt like it, usually to make Serena feel cowed if, in his opinion, she had been insufficiently docile.

One of his favourite put-downs was to remind her how middle-class her own background was. He reserved this criticism purely for her. Indeed, no-one could ever accuse Randolph of being a snob outside the home. Totally absorbed in his own myth, he never bothered to enquire about her own childhood, and the lovely Edwardian house she had grown up in. Had he done so, he might have released her own memories.

'Don't take your bitterness and failures out on me' she would retort. Yet when he became animated by drink, he would tell anyone who cared to listen that Serena was a breath of fresh air in his life, and that he worshipped the ground she walked on. She found these conflicting opinions very confusing.

The details he deigned to share of their new home in France were fairly sketchy. But Serena was fed up with the British climate and worn down by the constant effort of keeping mud out of her house. She had to admit that the warm south of France did seem enticing. She allowed herself to be persuaded into following his lead. She didn't think about it as thoroughly as she might have done, relieved that he seemed happier at the prospect. Later, she wondered why she hadn't considered the long-term ramifications for Sebastian and Scarlett. A furious Luke tried to take out a court order forbidding her to remove them from the UK, but as he had no intention of playing his part in helping to raise them, or educate them, he lost.

France Beckons

In 2001, many British, disenchanted with Tony Blair's Labour government, were flocking over the Channel to buy ridiculously low-priced houses in France. The weather was better, the wine cheaper, the way of life slower and more civilized, the food infinitely superior, and the French were just so unbelievably *chic,* they reasoned. In that sense, Randolph's decision was far from unique. Many others had bought the fantasy of a better life.

It was painful to leave. Sebastian and Scarlett had tearfully said goodbye to their schoolfriends at the end of term. Serena had parted from her parents equally tearfully, and yet she felt that it was both an adventure and a fresh start for them all.

On the deck of the ferry, to the shocked delight of the children, Randolph mooned at the white cliffs of Dover as they faded into the distance. How they all laughed as they anticipated their new exciting life. Bastille day – 14th July – found Serena motoring through France and gripping onto her car's steering grimly, as she tried to keep up with Randolph in the car ahead of her. Both vehicles were laden down with supplies for their first few days.

As they approached their promised land, the South of France wasn't looking quite so magical as she had been led to believe. The weather worsened to the point that she could barely see the road ahead. She narrowly avoided being killed outright on a sharp bend as an articulated truck ploughing through the filthy weather only just missed hitting them. 'The man must be a complete maniac' she snarled, yet to learn that this was the way the French habitually drove.

They arrived at a small village perched on a steep hillside, emerging from lowering grey clouds. The surrounding fields of sunflowers had deep brown sodden faces and were drooping from the rain lashing down on them. When they finally came to a halt, it was before a tall, severe looking house with blood red shutters. A nondescript black wrought iron grill covered a dreary, cheap front door, made of crazily glazed glass. When they eventually managed to unlock it the stench of cat pee nearly knocked her for six. Through the gloom the empty house silently challenged her. This was not at all what she had been expecting and she was completely bewildered. Her mobile phone went. It was the removal firm, informing her that they were running two days late – and then the line went dead.

The children were dazed and exhausted by the long journey and unable to take in their surroundings. 'Here we are then' announced Randolph, with a flourish. Serena ignored him and went to explore, desperate to find some redeeming features. In the sitting room stood an iron monster of a wood-burning stove. The kitchen contained an old-fashioned range also fuelled by wood. The downstairs loo was indescribably awful; it had bright orange walls and saloon-bar plastic doors. Up in the bedrooms they found only two old iron bedsteads with lumpy mattresses, smothered in lavender stalks. She was tempted to leave right there and then, but the children's wan faces stopped her in her tracks, and she had no idea where to go. For their sakes, she had to try and hide her dismay and make a go of things.

The next few days were grim. It was so cold that Randolph lit the log burner. They had no table, and no chairs, just the two horrible beds. Sebastian and Scarlett stared miserably out of the window at a small group of children hanging about in the village square. There were no shops, no bakery, and no bar; only narrow passageways and streets full of dog mess. Serena was totally dependent on Randolph to chop wood and steer her round the local supermarket, translating all the while. She was forced to subdue her simmering resentment, and after all, he wasn't responsible for the overdue arrival of their furniture.

Serena met their nearest neighbour when he fell out of his house clutching a plastic container of wine. His face was pock marked and ravaged by drink. He gave her a toothless leer and said something incomprehensible. Assuming it to be a greeting, she tried to reply, but he stared at her blankly. Randolph appeared and also spoke to him, but even he had was forced to admit that the strong southern accent was challenging. Darting back through her door, Serena burst into tears. She missed her home, she missed her family and friends and she absolutely hated the house. Eating her up inside was the realisation that she herself had nothing to run from, in leaving Britain. They were here entirely at Randolph's volition, because he needed to put his peculiar and mysterious past behind him. She would come to realise that it doesn't matter how many cupboards you try and hide your skeletons in; they will eventually reveal themselves.

One of the many promises that Randolph had broken, was to find somewhere with an outdoor space large enough to hold the children's beloved trampoline. Their rented house on the estate had a lovely garden, and this made it bearable. From her kitchen window, she'd seen them bouncing up and down without a care in the world. Friends would join them, and they would lie for hours happily staring up at the sky and chattering amongst themselves. When arriving home from school flushed and happy, they would fling aside their heavy school bags, wrench off their ties and escape to a world of their own. It was a real blow that there was no room whatsoever for a trampoline on a small and poorly constructed terrace.

'Plenty of other activities for them to occupy themselves with' was Randolph's dismissive response. Later, Serena wouldn't remember much about the time they spent in the house stinking of cat. She worked hard, scrubbing every inch of it, and when the summer finally arrived, spent long days painting it with soothing colours, trying to make it into a home.

A wealthy friend of Serena's with a holiday home in France came to call, and horrified by the way they were living, rushed her to the nearest Ikea. Serena had never visited one before and was taken aback by the idea of instant furniture. Everything conspired to make her feel that she was losing control of herself, and floundering in a strange country whose culture was alien to her. Randolph pointedly told her of an English woman living locally, who could help brush up her schoolgirl French. Unfortunately, this reminded her of being at school, not a good memory, for she had once been ridiculed by a frustrated and sadistic teacher. Any academic aspirations she might have had back then were knocked out of her. But the French teacher soon told her that she would never properly master the language and that she might as well give up and go home.

Serena found the north facing house with its hideous seventies' additions extremely depressing. In her eyes it hadn't the bones to become beautiful, needing far more than a lick of paint. She sat and pored over the property magazines but then Randolph announced that he had bought another house in the village as an investment without consulting her.

But he had underestimated Serena, who was determined not to stay in a house and a village that she loathed a moment longer than she had to. With an energy fuelled by fury, she set about dressing it for sale. She replaced the front door and whitewashed all the exterior walls. Blue and white check curtains lifted the gloomy windows and she decorated the terrace with bowls of fresh lavender and lemon bushes. Bright red geraniums filled faded terracotta pots. It made a pretty picture on a baking hot day when not a breath of wind stirred the sultry air.

An English couple looking for a holiday home made an offer immediately. They appeared not to notice the limitations of the village.

The Double Life

Randolph was now working away on a regular basis and totally consumed by his new job. They were forbidden to discuss the nature of this work with anyone. Serena had to train the children to give rehearsed and careful answers when schoolfriends asked what their stepfather did for a living. They were also told not to mention the countries to which he travelled, and Serena grieved that she was obliged to censor their natural desire to share stories about foreign lands. All three of them had to adopt code names when emailing or referring to each other in phone calls.

'Careless talk costs lives' he would quote sternly. 'I only impart information on a need to know basis, and the less you know, the less the risk to us all. I suggest you all do likewise', and so on and so forth. Serena almost expected him to issue them with gas masks...

He would come back from his month away completely wired. Immediately opening a bottle of chilled champagne, he would continue to drink all day and into the evening. After such an absence Serena was required to be ready and willing to resume marital relations. Simple in theory, but she found it difficult to adjust to his presence in her bed after several peaceful weeks alone.

The villagers viewed Randolph with a mixture of awe and suspicion, despite his apparent *bonhomie*. The children learnt to lie low when he first returned, then try to incorporate him back into their lives, but it was unsettling for them. It was particularly hard for Sebastian, who was changing from an outgoing confident teenager to a quieter, more withdrawn boy, who seemed nervous of his stepfather. They both desperately missed their grandparents, their friends, the diversity of the life they had known so well and speaking in their mother tongue.

Though they both made friends and could chatter away in French with ease, they were still conscious of being outsiders, and of a certain wariness.

The Riley

Randolph decided that it would be in keeping with his image as an English gentleman abroad to treat himself to a classic care. He had his eye on a vintage Riley, 'Just like the one my father used to tour Europe in', he informed Serena and went to England to complete the purchase and drive it to France.

The phone rang very early one morning. 'Put plenty of fizz on ice' he barked, 'we shall be arriving in an hour'. 'We' referred to his old friend Bertie who had decided to accompany Randolph back on his trip. In the past, he had confided to Serena the many ups and downs of his turbulent private life.

Sure enough, the tranquillity of the village was soon disturbed by the sound of a distinctly different car engine. Looking through the window as the Riley drew up, Serena gasped at her beauty. Lovingly built in 1951, her paintwork was a distinct and regal royal blue with a cream trim. Rushing out excitedly, she was greeted by two very weary faces.

'Absolutely shit journey, we need a drink badly', grumbled Randolph, omitting to kiss her. Ignoring him, she clambered aboard and instantly understood how a car could exude sex appeal. She inhaled the aroma of old red leather seats and felt their softness beneath her bare legs. Running her hands along the outline of the wide black steering wheel, she gazed at the assortment of dials on the maplewood dashboard. 'I think we may have fun in you' she murmured, and indeed they did.

Randolph had brought back lots of packs of English bacon, which they all missed as it was impossible to obtain in France. Serena laid the table and began to crack eggs as the first bottle was opened, the cork popping noisily and hitting the ceiling with a dull thud. It frothed over and was hastily divided between them. Randolph raised his glass, stood up, and proposed a toast.

'To the Grand Duchess' he declared, and this became the car's name. Breakfast was almost ready, and Randolph was opening a second bottle, when two sleepy children appeared in the doorway. They looked out of the window and down at the car in silence. They knew that the whole village would be intrigued by the unusual car that their eccentric stepfather had acquired and that they would be on the receiving end of curious questions. They didn't enjoy this but were becoming resigned.

The adults were hungrily attacking their bacon and eggs and working their way through the second bottle. Toast thickly spread with butter and marmalade had never tasted so good. Then Randolph began prodding Bertie to recount the latest events in his love life. Tongue now thoroughly loosened, he blurted out that he was currently being blackmailed by a young prostitute. Serena sat and contemplated the late middle-aged man in front of her, noting his thinning white hair and an expansive stomach. What did this old goat think he had going for him apart from money and power? She wasn't sure that she blamed the girl.

'How old is she?' asked Randolph and Serena hoped he wasn't going to say something approving. But on hearing the reply, he pulled a face.

'That's younger than my own daughters', Randolph said. He afterwards confided to Serena that he found the whole affair rather sordid. 'There are boundaries that even I wouldn't cross' he said. She preferred not to speculate quite where his own boundaries lay.

By the time the children left for school there was a curious little crowd gathered round the car, but no-one was daring to touch it.

But the excitement soon died down and Randolph was off on his travels again. Serena was left to her own devices. The house sale was proceeding satisfactorily, and she began to pore through property particulars. They were short on detail with some pretty appalling photographs but one of them caught her eye.

It was going to be a case of her heart ruling her head.

From Serena's Diaries

Does anyone ever forget that lurching feeling in the pit of the stomach when love at first sight makes you do something crazy?

I viewed Le Château on a hot July evening and entering the wide panelled hallway through the double glass inner doors I was instantly transfixed. In my mind's eye I had placed myself where I now sit writing this. Through the dusky gloom loomed an immense Louis Phillippe era staircase twisting enticingly up to the top floor. This beautifully proportioned Maison de Maître had lain untouched and unloved for many years.

Spacious rooms lined each side of the hallway. I could barely contain my excitement as the elderly owner showed me round. Who could resist double length windows, giving stunning views of the surrounding countryside? But I suppose the moment of no return came when I saw the ornate floor tiles and handsome panelling in the corridors. This was the beginning of a reckless love affair for which I take full blame.

I often wonder what it is that attracts people to houses that need enormous amounts of work, affection and money to restore them to their former glory. I'm also intrigued that people persist in persevering, even when it has become obvious that they have made a reckless decision.

When I began to research the history of Le Château, I found that we were only the third family in 200 years to have the privilege of living here. It was built in the early 1800's by a local landowner who doubtless chose the spot because of its outstanding views of the Pyrenees, and the neighbouring vineyards, which once belonged to the house. The outside of the house is plainer than the interior, as the owners did not wish to draw too much attention to themselves in unstable times following the French revolution.

Charmingly, each of the forty steps of the stairwell, is still numbered with the flourish of a pencil. The entire house is entirely metric, each room perfectly in proportion to its neighbours as in 1799 the metric measurement was introduced by two government surveyors. The roof space contained the servant's quarters and the remains of a circular contraption. It might have been an early attempt at air conditioning, or possibly a wind sail to capture any passing breeze in the summer heat.

The original family found other ways of finding refuge from the hot southern sun. The wooden panelling and shutters kept the house dark and cool. A field away lies the remains of what was once a bathing pool, the overflow from the spring feeding water back to the house. It is said that the entire village would enjoy a refreshing dip and it is certainly large enough, its proportions resembling those of an Olympic pool.

To the side of the house is a beautiful stone barn, older than the actual house itself and containing a pigeonnier. The only person in the village allowed the privilege of a pigeonnier was the squire himself, providing delicacies throughout the year for his family and guests. A lovely feature of the hallway is the positioning of a small marble basin. Sadly, the original tap is missing, but it would have provided immediate relief to the thirsty traveller, dismounting from his horse or carriage.

One of the most colourful stories from the past is the way in which the previous owner's grandfather came to possess the house. A descendant of the gentleman who built it incurred heavy gambling debts and the courts ordered that it must be sold to repay his creditors. A date was fixed for what was known as a 'candle auction' to take place in Le Château itself. All the interested parties would gather around a table containing a single lighted candle and watch the flickering flame as it burnt lower and lower. The bidding would begin as the candle wax and the wick began to splutter signalling that the flame was about to be extinguished. The buyers would hold their nerve and get their timing right, as the last bid put forward before the final flicker would seal the purchase.

Imagine the tension and anticipation as the candle was lit and the auction began.

I, of course, put my offer forward in a much more conventional style, though 'I'll pay the full asking price' is rapidly becoming outmoded, as the French property market becomes more depressed.

Serena has her Château

Randolph rushed back from Latin America alarmed by Serena's sudden decision to take on such a huge project. 'You haven't signed anything have you?' he asked, but it soon became clear that she would go ahead regardless. Once he had actually seen Le Château, he was noticeably less vocal. For a man who viewed himself as master of his own household, the term *Maison de Maître* had a rather obvious appeal.

Friends came to view the house, and as Serena had expected, were appalled yet fascinated.

'It's uninhabitable'

'It's a project too far'

and

'You really have lost it this time haven't you'?

Serena could picture the restored property in her mind's eye and she ignored them. There was certainly much to be done. The front door was barely a door at all, slowly rotting through years of neglect. When they stepped into one of the icy bathrooms to bathe you could see the stars through the roof despite there being an attic floor in between. Black holes in certain walls revealed hidden rooms, rickety staircases up to the attics were riddled with woodworm whilst the attics themselves were filled with layers of dust and dried husks of sweet corn laid down between the floorboards for insulation. The rats must have had a field day up there.

Sebastian and Scarlett were delighted that they were to have a whole floor to themselves. They could run and scream and shout and no-one would hear them. Their first winter there was bitterly cold, but they built fires in the huge fireplaces and huddled round them. They held Christmas in the kitchen where the tree stood alongside a large table and a sofa. It was just like an oversized bedsit. Most of the electricity wasn't yet working so they went to bed by torchlight. Dinner parties were also held in the kitchen after curious guests had done a candle-lit tour of the house.

The building was south facing so as the winter sun streamed through the front of the house, they all avoided the back. One particularly bright day Randolph decided to play host in The Grand Duchess, parked outside on the front drive. He and a couple of cronies, all dressed in English tweeds, were drinking aperitifs. A small group of villagers passing by stared and gasped at these weirdos.

Serena would take a break from her labours and ride her bike through the house, via the front door, along the corridor and through the back, take a turn to the right and peddle through the old stables and round to the front door to repeat the whole circuit. It was exhilarating, but it was also quite mad.

When the serious work began, it caused chaos. There were workmen everywhere, and the dust swirled around each room. When Serena decided to yield a sledgehammer one day no-one really noticed the wall come down. Randolph was away, and none too pleased to return and find that there was now a corridor between the master bedroom and bathroom where there had been a bricked-up room. 'I wanted a dressing room' was all she said.

There were tenants in the *apartement* above the garage. The agent had guaranteed that they would move on as soon as the purchase had gone through, but this of course was a lie. Though they paid a useful amount in rent, they clearly had no intention of going anywhere soon; even the disruption of the refurbishment wasn't going to shift them.

Serena despised them. They owned a large and ancient dog. Its mangy fur hung down off its haunches as it sat, leaning against the door frame for support. Come rain or shine it lived outside, a bowl of congealed spaghetti or other cheap muck in front of it, expecting little and receiving less. One day it was so bitterly cold that Serena couldn't bear to look out at the pitiful sight. She had previously tried to have a word about the poor animal's condition, but they regarded her a sentimental fool.

Snowflakes began to swirl around the dog as he stared blindly ahead. Next time she looked out, he had simply given up and keeled over. He lay there for a while until his body began to stiffen whereupon they came out, flung him into the back of the car and took him to the village *déchetterie*. You could go there and find plastic bags filled with kittens who had been drowned. French cruelty to animals sickened Serena, but she remained mute for fear of arousing hostility. She was alone much of the time and needed the goodwill of her neighbours.

Looking back, she wondered how she managed not to scream regularly. On a day when a digger truck was driving through the house, the noise was so horrendous that Serena curled herself up into a tight ball on a sofa and lit a fire. The deafening sound of a pneumatic drill as the workmen removed a deep cesspit to create a larger downstairs loo reverberated around the entire house. There was more mud inside the entrance to the house than there was in the garden itself.

Randolph didn't hang around to suffer the inconvenience of any of these alterations, jetting off to Latin America where he was for the most part unobtainable. When Serena protested, he would brusquely inform her that since it had all been her idea, she must see it through herself.

Basil

A stray dog had been sitting forlornly outside the local *huit a' huit* for some days now. After hearing Serena rage about the fate of her tenants' poor animal, her friend Lizzy urged her to rescue him. 'Otherwise he'll be put down', she said.

Making herself drive past the shop a few times she cast her eyes over the unfortunate creature. What she saw initially alarmed her. He was huge, and appeared to be a mixture of Beauceron, German Shepherd and Doberman. But when she plucked up courage to approach him, his tail thumped, and he gazed at her imploringly. She told Randolph that they must give him a home, and the children were thrilled.

The house was large, but Basil, as they decided to call him, seemed to fill the space quite easily. He was one hell of a dog and Serena was initially rather scared of him. They set out on their first walk. All went well until Randolph let him off the lead. She had never seen an animal run so fast. He tore through the undergrowth to the copse of trees by the roadside like a mad thing. His powerful charge stunned them both; he was not to be crossed that was for sure. 'You wouldn't break into the house with him on the other side of the door' a satisfied Randolph remarked. 'He'll make a fine guard dog. Just what we need'.

Basil did indeed bark whenever anyone approached the house, but more importantly he became Serena's loyal companion. The children adored him too; he was their gentle giant. Even her mother Evelyn, not a natural dog lover, tentatively stroked his head when she visited. He was almost her size and could easily have knocked her over. On the nights when Randolph was away, Basil would stretch his huge frame across her bedroom doorway, protectively. When she cried, he put his head in her lap sighing gently. He understood her, was completely devoted to her, and it was as though he knew he owed his life to her.

The Trip

Rather unexpectedly, since they hadn't been getting on at all well, Randolph announced that he was taking her on a trip.

'You'll be useful to me' was all he would say, refusing to reveal where they were going.

'Is it in this country'? she asked, though she secretly hoped for something more exotic. Possibly deliberately, Randolph left ticket stubs to all sorts of remote and tiny islands lying around for her to find. She had had to resort to Googling them to find out where they were. She couldn't see that they were anywhere near his stated destinations, but she didn't mention it and neither did he.

Before they left, Randolph bought an expensive new camera with a zoom lens. 'Learn to use it' he ordered. Serena was an enthusiastic photographer, so she didn't resent this as much as she should have done and was eager to try it out. And his final command was 'Do make an attempt to change your appearance, you look so bloody British'.

'That's because I am' she replied, 'What would you like me to look like? A blonde Scandinavian or a dusky south American like the ones on the dating sites you look at in secret?'. She stormed out of the room without waiting for an answer. He really was becoming nastier and nastier, but for the moment she was tied to the house by virtue of the renovations, and no escape route had yet presented itself to her.

She arranged for the children to be looked after and when they asked her where she was going, she responded with an embarrassed shrug and tried to pretend that it was to be a romantic surprise. They didn't say anything but looked at her reproachfully.

'You can always contact me by phone' she said apologetically but that was a tiny white lie as Randolph guarded their one mobile like a hawk. In the end she packed simple outfits that co-ordinated quite nicely with each another. He insisted she wear the Hermes scarf he had bought her, but she could never tie it satisfactorily. Conscious that it had cost him rather a lot of money she persevered with trying to achieve the *chic* effortless look that French women are supposed to possess although outside Paris, evidence of that was in short supply.

On the day of their departure, a powerful hire car with tinted windows arrived. It stuck out like a sore thumb in a tiny French village. Serena cringed inwardly; with his car, her car and The Grand Duchess they now possessed an embarrassing number of vehicles.

She bent down to embrace Scarlett and Sebastian. who had decided to feign indifference to her departure, although she suspected that they would miss her. Basil flung himself at her covering her clothes with his coarse hairs. Randolph carefully folded his Italian blazer and lay it on the back seat of the car. Glancing back, she was horrified to detect the sleek outline of a gun. She decided not to mention this yet; best to avoid a quarrel at the beginning of their journey.

They were seen off by Basil barking furiously he trotted behind them through the quiet village. 'Bloody animal,' Randolph grumbled, 'Can't you learn to control it'? His phone had started to ring, so she reached forward quickly to check the caller ID. It was her mother. She had tried unsuccessfully to call her earlier, needing the reassurance of the familiar voice before she went into unfamiliar territory. Randolph kept his eyes firmly on the autoroute ahead, his dark, slightly sinister looking glasses constantly masking his eyes, so that, disconcertingly, she couldn't see whether he was looking at her or not.

'I can't say where I'm going' Serena was saying to her mother, 'you know I can't'. Randolph's grip tightened on the wheel and she could tell he was becoming annoyed by the latest of many similar conversations.

'What's a normal life anyway'? Serena would always retort when her mother expressed concern about her unconventional circumstances. She supposed it was nice neat house with a patch of weed-free garden. A tarmac drive with a sparkling car that's religiously washed every Sunday morning whilst the weekend joint sits roasting in the oven? Tennis club membership, regular dinner dances at the stuffy club that a hard-working husband with half an eye on his younger secretary would take his neat quietly obliging wife to?

'Aren't they a happy couple?' people would whisper in admiration, wondering how he had kept his boyish good looks and she, her trim pre-baby figure. They wouldn't show themselves up by drinking too much and spending an entire day hungover. Serena sometimes tried to picture herself as such a woman, wondering whether this really was the path to contentment and joy, the two positive emotions that currently eluded her.

As this woman she would possess a tidy dressing table, displaying a collection of fragrant scents in pretty bottles. Semi-precious jewellery that her adoring husband had given on various anniversaries would be tucked away in a drawer, to pull out for special occasions. Later on, pictures of her children's graduations would jostle for space amongst wedding photographs and later still happy smiling images of her grandchildren would replace her own younger self, captured in time.

It would be orderly and serene this life of hers, an elegant descent into old age and then ultimately, a calm and happy release from her blameless life.

But it was not a life that she would ever lead.

'I'm not normal, mother' Serena firmly stated, and the stilted conversation drew to a close.

Randolph abruptly handed her a crisply folded map. 'Find Villeneuve' he instructed her, and she was suddenly faced with a confusing jumble of twisting roads and incomprehensible signs. Map reading simply wasn't her *forte*. It looked as though they would have to cut through a lot of back roads which would make the journey fairly arduous. She envisaged endless faceless villages where all the shutters would be tightly closed save for a solitary scruffy bar full of locals drinking beer and pastis, the ground littered with cigarette butts. Stray dogs of indeterminate breeding would lie under the cheap faded plastic tables baring their yellow teeth at the stray cats that dared approach too closely.

They did stop once at such a place *en route* and as she had guessed the bored customers regarded them with suspicion. The tables bore evidence of spilt sticky drinks. The older men were unshaven and shuffled between the bar and the tables in their worn-out espadrilles. The barman wore a greying sleeveless vest, the hairs under his arms thick with perspiration. Serena wondered out loud if there were any food available. 'Of course there will be.' stated Randolph contemptuously. 'This is *France,* the home of fine *cuisine*'. In the end the only snack available was a microwaved *Croc Monsieur*. Serena made a show of slowly chewing the rubbery sandwich whilst extracting long pieces of stringy cheese from her teeth. 'French cuisine my arse' she said under her breath. Randolph defiantly drank a *pastis* and rolled several cigarettes.

Eventually they reached their hotel and Serena was pleasantly surprised by it, as she surveyed the ornate façade. The shutters were painted her favourite colour of faded grey with the stonework the exact shade of pale pink roses after the rain. In certain circles, it was fashionable to stay here, and she discovered that the impressive oil paintings in the dining room were originals.

In their bedroom, the maid in her neat black and white uniform asked Serena in broken English if she would like her case unpacked, but Randolph intervened 'Parle Français si tu plais, Madame' he said warningly to Serena. 'Non-merci' she replied repressively.

'Why the hell not'? he said in amazement when the maid had left the room. 'Full of exciting new sex toys is it'? He laughed loudly at his own joke.

'No, but there's a fucking gun pressed against my toothpaste' she felt like retorting, but she didn't for fear of the possible repercussions. But feeling a little wobbly, she asked if they might order a drink. Randolph instantly produced a bottle of chilled bubbly from the mini-bar. 'No time like the present', he said and went in search of glasses.

Randolph was employed by an elderly millionaire, whose middle-aged wife was canoodling with a young playboy. She had just inherited a fortune from her late father which meant she was no longer dependent on her husband's money, so the millionaire was frantic to get some photographic evidence of her adultery.

Serena had done her homework beforehand and enjoyed the online images she had found of the beautiful young man. His life seemed to consist entirely of lounging around beautiful swimming-pools. She had silently congratulated the older woman on her good taste and that she had cocked a snook at those who sneered at the age gap.

Randolph's irascible client kept phoning from Paris, urging action. He had just heard that a friend had glimpsed his wife and her lover walking along La Promenade des Anglais in Nice. They knew roughly where the couple were based, in a rented villa tucked away in the folds of the hills, some distance from the garish lights of the casinos and overpriced restaurants overlooking the harbour.

They parked the car in a road lined with high security gates and intercoms. Occasionally a white van emblazoned with the logo of a gardening or pool cleaning service would remind them that their own part of France was yet to become fashionable enough to attract the very rich. They ambled along, searching for the right address. 'We can discount the old git's own villa, since she's hardly likely to be playing away at home, is she'? Randolph remarked. 'Oh, I don't know, your own lady friends seemed to manage' she replied thinking of Randolph's past flings with married women, and barely suppressing a laugh.

'Take this a little more seriously' he hissed, 'Once the old git has his evidence, that dirty little nobody shagging like some stray dog on a street corner will disappear.' As Serena digested these words, she felt a wave of sympathy for the couple. But it was a job; if they didn't do it someone else would, and they needed the handsome fee.

Thick glossy evergreen leaves put hostile barriers between them and the view of the houses. 'Fancy living like a prisoner' she remarked, thinking of her own glorious house with its open drive and uninterrupted views. Once they had scoured the nameless roads, they took the car further afield and surveyed the properties from a distance. Suddenly Serena saw it, the long blue pool reached by wide stone steps, each one embracing a fat clay pot full of vivid tumbling red geraniums, borders ablaze with carefully nurtured lavenders. A few figures were crouched on the perimeters, tidying the borders and a slight woman was sweeping away the fallen pine cones from the terraces.

Serena took out her camera and fiddled with the zoom lens, homing in on a man wearing a battered straw hat. She could see his weathered face and clicked off a few shots whilst he sat down in the shade and rolled a cigarette. 'It's a bloody brilliant camera' she remarked, focusing on the field awash with poppies that lay between the road and the property. Their view of the house and grounds blurred slightly in the heat of the day. The piercing blue Mediterranean lay behind them and the hum of the ceaseless traffic on the coastal road sounded like the harmless voice of a bee from this distance.

As they watched, two figures strolled onto the terrace in the direction of the lawn. Randolph was instantly alert and gestured to Serena to pay attention. It was the lovers, holding hands. The woman was tastefully dressed in a loose white gown. As Serena raised the camera again, she admired the gigolo's lithe yet muscular body. She crouched down to steady herself and through the viewfinder, she could see a group of men dressed entirely in black, hovering behind the couple.

'Now all we need is to get a few shots of some fruity action round the poolside, the old boy will be satisfied, and we can go and find somewhere decent for lunch' murmured Randolph. But just then they caught the glint from a pair or raised binoculars. 'Get down' snapped Randolph, opening the car's bonnet and leaning over the engine in studiedly forensic manner. Taken by surprise Serena lost her balance, toppled onto the grass verge and was promptly bitten by an insect; it throbbed for days.

'Pictures' he hissed at her from his hiding place. She rose painfully and pointed the camera towards the sloping lawns. As she clicked away, the couple entwined their bodies and kissed, and the bulky men in black turned away. In the shimmering heat-haze they almost appeared to be dancing their way towards the swimming pool, shedding their outer garments in an expensive trail of linen. An upright butler followed them, with a tray containing an ice-bucket and glasses. On the terrace, staff were laying the table for lunch in the shade of a vine-covered trellis. The woman, who was very trim for her age, Serena noticed, submerged herself in the water as her admirer sat on the edge on the steps of the pool chatting to her. She laughingly put her head between his thighs.

'Dear god' muttered Randolph muttered, as if in disgust. Serena felt a stab of envy mingled with respect. This seemingly mismatched pair were totally at ease with their bodies and each other. She could well imagine the jealous reaction of Randolph's contact when he received these images. The dining table was now laid, its cloth moving slightly in the breeze, and the staff had retreated indoors. Serena snapped away, fully focused on the task in hand. The black-clad men were now talking amongst themselves in a huddle. Through her lens she could see a pleasing line of dark hair running down his torso as he stood up and prepared to dive into the water. He raised his arms tucking his head down, knees bending slightly when something whistled through the air. He fell forward into the water. Before she could take this in, two huge dogs were heading towards her at a furious speed, barking hungrily. viciously as they homed towards their prey. She was paralysed with fear, but Randolph grabbed her arm urgently, looking as shocked as she felt.

'There's an invisible electronic barrier' he said, 'it will freak them' and as if by magic they appeared to be thrown back in the air as their pursuit was thwarted. Randolph pushed her roughly into the car, but rather than driving off like a bat out of hell, pulled the motor smoothly out of the parking spot and continued along the road at a moderate speed. Serena stared blindly ahead of her, unsure quite what she had witnessed. After a few kilometres, they heard the wail of sirens and coming from the opposite direction, two blue vans full of *gendarmes* coming from the opposite direction hurtled past them.

'Poor fucker' Randolph murmured, 'God knows what happened back there. Let's go have a drink, I think we've earnt one.' He patted her knee, and her eyes filled with tears. But all she said was 'Yes, let's.'

Serena never discovered quite why the handsome playboy had fallen forwards into the pool and she was too afraid to ask any questions. Yet the muscular outline of his body its unnatural twitching during his aborted dive invaded her dreams for months afterwards.

But she did begin to question the life she was leading. Careless of convention from her teens onwards, she had instinctively responded to Randolph's policy of living on the edge. Theirs was not a conventional marriage in that they weren't in a financial position to look too far ahead and make plans.

Yet whilst she acknowledged this, a voice in her head was urging her to jump off the carousel, climb down from the roller-coaster ride. But she couldn't see a way to do this without huge upheaval for Sebastian and Scarlett, who were now accustomed to life in France.

She was simply in the wrong place at the wrong time.

Spanish Declarations

Randolph's absences became more frequent and more shrouded in mystery. When he returned, the atmosphere was uneasy and awkward. Though evasive about his own activities, he cross-questioned everyone else about theirs, and showed resentment that they were able to manage without him.

He began goading Serena constantly, telling her in front of the children that she was in every way an inadequate wife. Keen as ever to play the lord of the *Manoir,* he constantly issued invitations to dinner parties which they could ill-afford to give, and then belittled her in front of friends, knowing that she would not retaliate in company. Instead, she retreated further and further into her inner life.

Until recently, they had one communal PC, which sat on Serena's desk in the restored library. It was on the first floor overlooking the vineyards, and in winter, the snow-capped peaks of the Pyrenees. To exercise her mind and simultaneously drum up interest in their area, Serena had begun a blog about Le Château and it had found a small but appreciative audience.

Randolph derided her grammar and spelling, but in company he would say loudly 'No-one admires Serena as much as I do'. He had recently acquired a laptop, and moved his own desk behind hers, to keep an eye on what she was posting and mask his own online activities. By now suspicious, Serena had no compunction in accessing his email account on the PC, which she reckoned he wasn't sufficiently computer literate to have hidden.

She wasn't sure what she had expected to find, but messages featuring cuddly bears and love hearts appeared onscreen. Serena's Spanish was rudimentary but even she couldn't mistake the meaning of '*te amo, querido*'. Randolph's replies were couched in equally loving terms. She felt weirdly lightheaded and the room seemed to spin around her. Randolph was sitting reading at his father's leather topped desk, surrounded by his books, all beautifully shelved by subject and in alphabetical order by Serena; a labour of love for a two-faced bastard.

She turned her chair around, got shakily to her feet and stood over him.

'Are you having an affair?' she asked bluntly. He looked up in bewilderment, caught off guard and uncertain how to deal with such a direct question. Serena went over to the computer and pointed towards all the red hearts filling the screen. 'I'll ask you one more time' she said, 'Are you having an affair?'

He looked back at her coolly. 'Yes' he replied, 'Are *you*? She was so incensed that without thinking, she replied that she was.

'There you go, then' he said, 'We're quits'. And he calmly went back to his book.

Rooted to the spot, Serena stared at the man who was her husband, her vision still filled with the ghastly teddy bears. Then she laughed in disbelief. 'You're quite pathetic' she said and turned back to her own computer. There was an awkward silence that hung in the air which prompted her to begin to tap on her keyboard furiously. She logged on to an airline website and began looking at flights back to England.

'Now what are you doing'? Randolph said, sounding alarmed.

'I'm getting a one-way flight back home' she replied, 'and you can go fuck yourself'. He stood up abruptly, knocking the chair over in his haste. Putting his fingers to his lips, he signalled to her to keep quiet, whilst he bent and ran his fingers on the underside of the desk. Then he gestured to the car outside, so urgently that she followed him unquestioningly.

They both climbed into the newly acquired BMW which lay gleaming and immaculate on the drive. It was another of Randolph's ostentatious acquisitions, designed to create the illusion that they were fabulously wealthy, although it mostly further alienated the villagers. Randolph's eye's narrowed as he fired up the powerful engine. Serena looked out of the window at the ancient and twisted olive tree which she had planted so hopefully just after they had moved in. Despite her anger, the thought of leaving the house which she had turned into a stylish home dismayed her. She opened her mouth to berate him further, but he told her to shut up. The car roared up a steep hill into an ancient village. The panoramic vantage point made a suitably dramatic spot for a heated exchange. Randolph got out of the car and gestured for her to do likewise.

'Christ' Serena said, 'you always make such a bloody drama of things'. He enveloped her in his arms and ran his fingers through her hair.

'Serena, I'm only in love with you' he said, 'there's no-one else, surely you must know that'?

'No, I *don't* know that, and I'm going back to England' she shouted. 'I am just so exhausted by your constant carping and criticism, your stupid games and heartily sick and tired of all your crappy stories'.

Randolph signed deeply and sank down onto a low stone wall which ran around the perimeter of the viewing area. In the distance the tops of the Pyrenees lay glistening, the winter snow sharpening their outline against the sky. Below them, Serena could see the empty fields which any day now, the farmers would sow with sunflower seeds. In the summer there would be row upon row of blazing yellow heads. It was a lovely place, she thought wistfully, as she wondered what drivel he was about to feed to her. So she attacked first.

'I'm surprised at you' she began 'teddy bears and love hearts are hardly your style'. 'They aren't my style at all' he retorted 'as you well know'. 'The messages are cover for my work. I must have a believable reason to go in and out of the country so often, you ought to know that, and a fake romance has worked well. You *have* to believe me; my job involves things which could possibly place all our lives in danger. The last thing I need right now is for you to kick up a fuss. I'm simply trying to protect us all the best I can'.

'Bloody hell' she snorted, 'you certainly know how to spin one don't you'?

Randolph looked affronted. 'So who are you having an affair with anyway'? he shot at her.

'I'm not' she replied sulkily, 'but I might just consider it'. There had been a couple of missed opportunities whilst he had been away. It might have lessened her isolation, stuck as she was in a village devoid of social life, though she was the first to admit that she was responsible for their location.

'Well, why the hell did you say you were, then'? he demanded, 'Because *you* did' she snarled. But she knew that he had somehow gained the upper hand. As she had no hard facts, she could not dispute his story. 'Well that's cleared that up' he said smugly. 'Apparently, neither of us are having an extra-marital fling'.

Then his tone of voice changed. 'But you really must be careful' he said seriously. 'I think the phones are being bugged, maybe even the car, who knows?' He spread his hands out at looked down at his knuckles. 'Don't talk to anyone openly whilst I am away and keep the doors locked. The dog will frighten anyone off anyway. Tell the children to use their code names always on the phone and on the internet and don't write anything to me of a personal nature, no names, no places, no details. I don't know if 'they' would track you down directly to the house, but you never know'. His words hung menacingly in the space between them'.

Serena got into the BMW and sank back into the plush cream leather interior. When they drove up to the house, she feasted her eyes on its façade, appraising everything that had been done. She walked through the hallway and into the walled garden and even in winter it pleased the eye. It had been artfully landscaped around a stunning swimming pool. In the fierce heat of the summer, fig trees shaded its edges and pots of bright red geraniums placed seemingly haphazardly would bloom riotously. In one corner, they had planted an enormous palm tree. In another hidden spot Serena's childhood hammock would hang from a tree whilst the church clock chimed prettily on the hour. They had planted up hundreds of daffodils and tulips on the steep banks, apple and pear trees had been trained against walls. Some mornings, if there was the hint of spring in the air it was impossible not to relish this lovely place.

Serena remembered swimming alone the previous summer, her worries seeming to float away. She would climb out of the pool and tip toe through the handsome double glass doors and into the cool of the panelled hallway. In the inlaid marble washbasin there was always a glorious vase of flowers, picked from the garden. One thing they agreed on was that a home without flowers or greenery was unloved and unfinished. The sun's rays would make shafts of dusty light fall upon the ancient patterned tiles in hues of pale and deep grey. The warmth emanating from the cream four door Aga would hit her as she reached her spacious south facing kitchen. Low double windows looked out over the vineyards and the mountains beyond.

Basil would greet her by throwing his substantial and powerful body against her thighs. Back in the here and now, she wondered whether she really could turn her back on all this loveliness, everything she had worked so hard to restore? After all, it was mainly her creation although Randolph had concurred with her choices happily enough. She tried to imagine what there would be to go back to. How could she uproot the children once more, slinking back to an uncertain future, fleeing from a failed marriage and a failed adventure?

It was unthinkable. She would just have to put up and shut up. Shuddering slightly, she dismissed an image of herself as a bird, hopping around in a gilded cage with the door firmly closed.

Serena trailed up the vast stone staircase and into her bedroom. Last night's fire still smouldered in the fireplace. She carefully withdrew a small locked box from its hiding place next to the bed and inhaled deeply the sweet-smelling home grown weed. Tiptoeing up to the attics where she knew he was unlikely to try and follow she sat down on one of the old wooden wine boxes and rolled herself a small joint. The end flared briefly when she lit it and she took a couple of small puffs, just enough to give her a little hit and take the edge off her uneasy suspicions.

Making her way carefully down the rickety wooden staircase she snorted with derision as she recalled the old ham hung up to dry in that room when she had first viewed the house. The windows had been covered with thin wire mesh rather than glass to let the air in. She had laughingly asked the owner's wife if the ham was included in the sale, but the old crone had thrown her such a look of horror at the very idea that she realised that she would never understand the mentality of these people.

By the time Serena had reached the ground floor and entered the kitchen she was flying nicely. Randolph had opened a bottle of wine to deflect her and avoid any awkwardness. 'Ah' he said smoothly, 'I'm glad you've calmed down and seen sense'. Sanctimonious bastard, she thought. She put on some loud music and started dancing and singing to herself. Randolph began to look distinctly amorous. She knocked back several glasses of wine, relishing its numbing effect. She drank more, so that later, in their bedroom, she let him do what he wanted without protest. She was beyond caring...

With the morning came a hangover and depression. She knew, really, that she was fighting a losing battle. Some close friends of Serena's, Sophie and Nick, had recently visited from England, talking long into the night after Randolph had gone to sleep. Sebastian and Scarlett had opened their hearts to this couple, begging them to speak bluntly and tell Serena how much they hated seeing her humiliated day after day, losing confidence and shrinking before their eyes. Sophie was also appalled that Randolph could still find the funds to drive around The Grand Duchess and take out a loan on the BMW. As an astute businesswoman she was worried that he was overstretching himself, just as he had in England. Serena herself had almost ceased to notice, because if you are drip fed poison daily in small doses you gradually become inoculated against just that insidious drip.

Of course, it was lovely to have friends to stay and Randolph continued on his merry, if irresponsible way, playing *le grand seigneur* with his customary nonchalance. But there was no denying the awkward tension between them. And to her dismay, Sebastian and Scarlett were gradually distancing themselves, avoiding speaking to him unless strictly necessary. Worst of all, they now refused to eat supper at the same table as their stepfather, taking their meals elsewhere. Serena felt terribly conflicted, as her beloved children became watchful and silent.

Drugs

On one such evening the guests were becoming raucous. Randolph was opening another bottle. He paused theatrically and bent his head towards the newly pulled cork. 'This is a particularly fine burgundy' he announced, with a satisfied smirk.

Just then, one of Sebastian's friends appeared at the front door, an awkward figure nervously peering into the house and shy of the noisy gathering. He asked for Scarlett, who came downstairs. They talked briefly, in rapid French, and then he melted back into the darkness of the night. Scarlett came into the dining-room, pale with horror. She came to stand by Serena and said haltingly 'Sebastian's been arrested'.

The table fell silent whilst everyone digested this piece of information. Serena was stunned. 'What in god's name for? she asked. 'Possession of drugs' mumbled Scarlett unhappily. Serena leapt to her feet, but Randolph grabbed her arm and said viciously 'Let the little fucker rot in the cell for the night, it'll do him good and sober him up'.

Serena turned on him furiously. Words tumbled from her, slightly incoherent and jumbled, but leaving him in no doubt that his attitude disgusted her. One of the guests signalled to her partner that they must leave. They downed their glasses with indecent haste and excused themselves on the grounds that couldn't associate themselves with drug users. Supposedly a devout Catholic, she would later turf her own son out of her house leaving him to scavenge around the village bins for food. But a friend who was well over the limit stood up. 'Come on' he said, 'let's go and rescue him'. Randolph simply turned his back and poured himself another drink.

The drive into town was a nightmare, a long tunnel of lethal plane trees passed Serena in a blur. When they arrived at the police station the lighting was harsh. They were treated with disdain and forced to endure a lecture on the dangers of pot before they were told what had happened. Sebastian and several friends had been sitting in a stationary car smoking and the *gendarmes* had pulled up to investigate. Unluckily, Sebastian was sitting on the bag of weed, so was deemed to be the ringleader. The local Mayor was a narrow-minded bigot with a zero-tolerance approach to drug use which he insisted that the police implement. Unsympathetic to the bored and disaffected youngsters in the area, he refused to grant permission for a football pitch. When one boy was seen entering the village hall clutching a bottle of vodka, he immediately closed it down, leaving them with nowhere to hang out. It was hardly surprising that they huddled together in someone's car.

But Serena knew she must bite her lip if she wanted Sebastian released. After further warnings, they were allowed to see him and after paying a fine, he was released. He was exhausted and on the verge of tears, so Serena took him in her arms lovingly, watched impassively by the *gendarme*. When they got back to the house, Randolph was still carousing with his insensitive friends. Serena turned on her heel and went to bed.

The next morning, Serena and the children were peremptorily summoned to the kitchen. Randolph stood with his back against the Aga warming himself, but his face was ashen with rage and hangover. He was curt and to the point.

'Either he goes, or I do.'

Clearly, he believed he could frighten Serena into agreeing but he had underestimated her loyalty to her son.

'Let me help you pack your bags then' she replied. Thwarted, he raked up Serena's youthful experiments with soft drugs. 'Your judgement is seriously impaired' he bellowed, ' and your brain is shot to shit by all those years of drug abuse'. He was exaggerating for effect but, reflected Serena, he didn't know what he was talking about and wasn't averse to taking a sneaky puff himself. 'Pot, kettle, black' she shot back at him.

To make matters worse, the menopause had just kicked in and Serena felt wretched. The mood swings didn't help her domestic situation. Occasionally she would completely lose it with Randolph, who seemed to delight in goading her. Despite his own drinking habits, every time she poured herself a comforting glass of wine at the end of a hard day, he would say that she was a borderline alcoholic. Or he would sneer 'You really are unstable you know; you should go and see the doctor and be referred for help'.

It was a huge relief to them all when at the end of the month he flew off to work again. Terrified by the way that their debts were mounting up, Serena had, with some success, begun to take in paying guests, for bed and breakfast. But money was still flowing out faster than it was coming in. Randolph would insist on borrowing substantial amounts from the bank, to keep them just slightly ahead of their creditors. And there had been more signs that he was leading a double life. She found receipts to hotels, two to three days spent in tiny offshore islands on both the outward and return journeys. She could seldom get hold of him if there was an emergency of any kind. 'Just deal with it' he would say when they did have sporadic conversations. She now mistrusted everything that he said to her. And once trust is gone, a meltdown becomes inevitable.

Randolph would now respond to emails when he was home. 'You're supposed to be home to switch off' she would protest, but he would sharply tell her to mind her own business. She was worn down by the hard work it took to run the house and her growing business. He was never any practical help though he enjoyed drinking with the guests. Her closest friends were horrified by his arrogance and increasingly bizarre behaviour. Pictures of sultry young women with their arms wrapped around him now appeared on his laptop, and he left love letters written in childish handwriting for her to find.

After one trip, Serena picked up a wooden set of dominoes and remarked that she hadn't seen them before. 'They are a present from a very dear friend of mine' he informed her, 'and whilst we are on the subject, I should tell you that I intend to adopt her, legally'. Serena gaped at him in astonishment. Had she heard him correctly? Apparently, she had. 'All the adoption papers are in place' he continued blandly, as if this was the most normal thing in the world. He had met her widowed mother and they were eager for the procedure to go ahead. She wanted a father figure, he said, though she wasn't a child, it transpired, but a woman in her twenties. 'She wants a bloody sugar daddy, you mean' shouted Serena, beside herself with anger.

Sadly, the children overheard this. A distraught Scarlett ran out of the house with the dog and disappeared, but Sebastian caught up with Serena as she stormed outside to her car, close to tears. Looking completely bemused, he jumped in the passenger seat. Serena drove straight over the house of a friend who practiced as a psychiatrist although she seldom spoke about her work. She sat patiently and listened to what they both had to say. Then she gently took Serena's hand. 'Leave him before he destroys you all', she advised. 'It won't be easy, but you will never regret it'.

Returning home, Serena began flinging their belongings into suitcases. Though she tried to ignore him, Randolph hovered over her talking agitatedly. 'You will never understand the South American people; their passion, the tight family ties, the commitment these proud people make to those they love' he said, 'You're just so damned middle-class and uncultured'.

There was a term for his bewildering conduct. Randolph was a narcissist and when she came to understand that everything made perfect sense.

Fate Intervenes

Fate immediately intervened. The phone rang, and it was Serena's mother with bad news.

'Darling, I'm afraid your father has had a stroke, you should come over immediately'.

Beside herself with worry, Serena caught the first available flight. Though her heart was breaking it was nothing to the pain she felt when arriving at the hospital, she found her father looking ill and shaken. He was trapped in a public ward, next to a man suffering from mental illness, who was noisy and disruptive. He would scream and threaten to kill everyone.

'Come on' he would say to her father, 'we're going to fight them all, we'll get into a proper scrap and beat the hell out of them'. All Serena's father could do was to nod weakly and helplessly close his eyes. Sitting by his bedside, Serena reflected that she was sick of fighting everyone herself. Every time she phoned home Sebastian was sullen and resentful. She could feel him pulling further and further away from her. Randolph pretended to be sympathetic, but she knew he would be thrilled to be left to his own devices, separated by the Channel from the 'harridan' as he now called her.

When her father was finally out of danger and discharged to be cared for by her mother, Serena reluctantly left England. She knew that her place was with her children. Even so, she dreaded what she would find at home, and it was typically bizarre. To facilitate his double life, Randolph had moved himself into a caravan in the cavernous garage and taken with him his most precious possessions, rather like a squirrel hoarding for the winter. There were piles of musty smelling books, overflowing ashtrays, empty glasses stained with cheap red wine. Whenever she ventured to criticise him, he would shout at her that he had had enough of her mental abuse.

Serena and the children did their best to ignore him, trying not to let his eccentricity affect them. They stopped bringing friends home, but people no longer wished to visit them anyway, presumably thinking the form of madness was contagious. Serena phoned her parents daily, offering them support and clinging on to their expressions of concern for her. But eventually, and in a desperate attempt to lessen the conflict raging through the house, she took Randolph back into the matrimonial bed.

Sebastian had become a shadow of his former self. His handsome face was now gaunt and there were huge black circles under his eyes. He was rarely at home and small amounts of money and inconsequential items went missing, and although it might have been the children of one of their guests with light fingers, Randolph had no hesitation in accusing him of theft. The atmosphere was intolerable and after a particularly unnecessary snide comment had been aimed at Serena, Sebastian lost his temper and went for Randolph, aiming a punch at him.

Launching herself between them, Serena begged them to stop. She couldn't take any more and found herself sobbing and shaking hysterically, prompting Scarlett to phone the doctor. He immediately prescribed a course of sedatives. She was happy to take anything that would temporarily lift her from the continuing agony of a family torn apart. And things were getting worse and worse. There was an emergency visit to the hospital one morning after she had found Sebastian shaking uncontrollably on his bed one morning. His body had become skeletal. Randolph was completely devoid of compassion. 'The boy's a complete piss ant' he would snort.

Leap into the Unknown

Randolph, Serena and Scarlett were sitting in the kitchen one night when the most horrendous banging came from upstairs. It sounded as though furniture was being thrown around in a frenzy.

'He's trashing his bedroom' Serena screamed in alarm, petrified for her son. 'I'm calling the police' Randolph fumed, 'I've simply had enough of his shit'. Serena heard thumping and turned to him ashen faced, 'He's opening the attic windows'. Her heart froze; it sounded as if he was climbing out onto the lethally high roof. He must be absolutely stoned out of his mind. The three of them rushed outside but it was so dark that they simply couldn't see the roof.

Scarlett's phone rang out shrilly, she answered it and then let out the most terrifying primal scream whilst sinking to her knees and moaning loudly. 'Nooooo'. The words split Serena open to the core. She was crazy with fear as she ran inside and took the stairs two and three at a time, howling his name repeatedly and praying. 'Dear god, dear god *please* don't do this to me'.

The door was locked, and she frenziedly kicked it open, splintering it as she did so. As she had feared, the room was in ruins but of Sebastian there was no sign. Rushing to the window she looked out fearfully. But then she heard a faint whimpering sound from a deep cupboard and wrenching open the door, she found him cowering in a corner, a broken boy. She fell to her knees her body belt double under the weight of her grief. How had it ever become so bad?

Financial Meltdown

It had been inevitable for some time, but they now went into total financial meltdown. Threatening letters began to arrive from the bank and started to pile up in an alarming fashion. Randolph ignored them all. He disappeared, conveniently called away and uncontactable. Serena was left alone to face the music.

Hearing Basil barking furiously, she came downstairs one day to discover a group of men huddled together in her hallway. She didn't like the way they were looking through open doors, and two of them were threateningly stocky and muscular. One of them was clutching a clip-board and looked up as she approached, eyeing her coldly. He introduced himself as the local *huissier*, or bailiff. He served her with a piece of paper which he insisted she sign. It listed the debts which Randolph had not deigned to refused to acknowledge. 'You have just two weeks to pay' he said brusquely, and they left. Bloody hell she was being given a fourteen-day deadline.

She called the children, and they held a council of war at the kitchen table. Casting around for a solution, Serena announced that they were relocating next door. The tenants in the *apartement* over the garage had recently left, and although the loss of their rent had been regrettable, they at least had a refuge. 'Pack up your rooms now' she said 'and I'll turn off the Aga'.

It took them the whole afternoon to move the basics in, but by the evening she had lit a small fire in the kitchen of their new home and they felt cosy enough. Tired though she was, she sat down at the PC and began to work on the marketing of the château. It would be a luxury holiday let for up to fourteen people. After a week of intensely hard work she had a website up and running, and their major personal possessions had been removed. There was an interconnecting door between the main house and the *apartement*. Serena felt like Alice in Wonderland stepping through the looking glass into one life from another. Her new bedroom overlooked the garden and the pool, and had French windows leading onto a terrace. In the distance she could see the famous Canigou mountain and the distinctive red tiles of the village roofs.

By her actions, Serena managed to appease the *huissiers* for some time. The rental of the château turned out to be profitable and successful. She would sit for hours on the computer building an online presence, taking all her own photographs and writing about the experience of staying in an unusual house. She also increased her blogging activity. She felt herself blossom as she began to earn the extra money that they so badly needed.

Above the *apartement* was another enormous attic space which Randolph commandeered as his own when he returned from South America. As it was only accessible by a steep metal ladder perched precariously against a wall, no-one else entered his domain. Though he claimed to profess admiration for Serena's efforts, he was still secretive and remote, though Serena found that she didn't care as much as she had. They were no longer in love and her priority was to keep a roof over her children's heads.

Le Mayor

Randolph loved nothing more than to argue and Serena wasn't the only target. He became involved in a dispute over land attached to a second house he had owned in their former village. Serena had managed to sell the building privately, but a neighbour had subsequently claimed that the land belonged to him. Naturally Randolph decided to fight back, on a point on principle. The Mayor of that village had assured him that they simply couldn't lose the case. Eventually, they paid more in legal fees than the house was originally worth, after several years of wrangling in court. Randolph relished the fight, but Serena didn't. They couldn't sue their *notaire* for incompetence, and under the French legal system there was no system in place for a reassessment. It simply didn't exist.

When their adversary had visited the house to complain, he rudely stuck his middle finger up in the air. Randolph had responded by bending his finger backwards and telling him to 'go forth and multiply'. This scarcely endeared him to the locals.

Despite being badly bitten Randolph, then thought a difference of opinion with the mayor of their current village might provide some harmless sport. Le Château was surrounded by stunning countryside, and so far, the village had retained its unique charm. It was one of many distinctive small villages dating back to medieval times, and offered an unchanged slice of French rural life, which draws tourists to the Languedoc. To walk out of the front door of the château and straight onto open glorious land was a privilege. At night time there was no light pollution of any kind and they would stare up at the milky way and millions of stars on clear nights. Shooting stars would burst briefly whilst the dog would run around them joyfully.

The Mayor, Jean-Claude had done a cunning deal under the table by selling off land that lay adjacent to the château to a developer. It was all above board in theory, but many of the villagers didn't bother to question the deal too much, as they were paid off handsomely if the development was likely to encroach on their own land. There were rumblings of discontent amongst the more prominent and educated villagers and clandestine meetings took place in private homes. Naturally, Randolph voiced his opinions loudly, and vowed to speak out at the public meeting which was going to be held. He wrote letters of objection, openly signing them. Serena was deeply perturbed by this and feared that there would be repercussions.

'No good will come of this' she protested. 'Why can't you just lie low for once?' but of course he ignored her.

The evening of the meeting arrived. Everyone who has promised to attend was there, but instead of standing up and querying the underhand nature of the land sale, they remained passive. Only Randolph got to his feet. He made a highly dramatic speech in which he spelt out his objections, and Jean-Claude stormed out, spluttering with rage. Serena didn't attend the meeting. She had already decided that she wanted to leave. She hadn't moved here to live next door to a development of cheap nasty characterless houses each one surrounded by a prissy privet hedge. Her love affair with the château and rural France was well and truly over.

Ironically, Jean-Claude would be soon stepping down from office. He had served his term, lining his own pocket and would slip away quietly, before becoming accountable for ruining the village forever. But he had one last sneaky trick up his sleeve.

A week later, Randolph and Serena were standing on the terrace overlooking the sweep of the drive when the deputy mayor marched up to the front door. He was a factious little man, ex-military and chippy. Now a policeman, he had been a sneering presence on the night of Sebastian's arrest. By this time most of the village suspected that Randolph was a spook, and he did little to disabuse them of this impression. His tongue would loosen dangerously as he drank more and more, embroidering his stock of stories. Pinning a note to the front door, the bureaucrat scurried away.

Serena went down to investigate and found a slim waterproof envelope with an official wax seal. Inside was a formal notice signed by Jean-Claude. He was officially instructing Serena to close her business on the grounds that she had breached a regulation so tiny that it took her breath away. It seemed that if you were offering self-catering accommodation, you could only rent out five bedrooms. The château, and many other similar properties had more, but the way everyone else overcome this, she was later told, was to *admit* to offering just five.

They say that revenge is a dish best served cold and Serena knew that Randolph's attack had triggered this devastating development. But the nightmare didn't end there. Even when officially retired, the ex-mayor was so in cahoots with the local police that he leant on them to make regular visits to check that Serena was not trading illegally.

They would turn up randomly, in a large van. Swaggering around the drive in their high leather boots, guns in holsters, they would peer at the closed shutters. Possibly disappointed that she was not trading illegally they would retreat, titillating the villagers, who were not above whispering that they had only got their comeuppance.

Serena mourned the death of her business, and the stress of feeling powerless threatened to break her.

Fly Away

Serena had loyal and supportive friends who were on her side as she struggled with the enormity of it all. And she needed them. Relations with Randolph had become so frosty that after he had announced he was going away again, she deposited him at the airport drop off point, unwilling to prolong their goodbyes. But he insisted on having the last word.

'I am leaving for a month' he announced 'on a job that is dangerous and lonely. The very least you could do is show me some affection. You may live to regret your coldness; one day I might not return...' Yet another example of the emotional blackmail of which he was a master.

'And you could show me some fucking respect' Serena stormed.

'Must you use the language of the gutter?' he retorted disdainfully. 'If applied properly, English is a marvellously flexible and nuanced language which can be used to convey all sorts of subtle reactions and responses. Indeed,' he continued, as he lifted his luggage from the back seat 'it is only vulgarians who cannot fully appreciate the beauty of our mother tongue and at the same time control their vile temper'. And he slammed the car door shut.

'Fuck off' she shouted again, putting her foot on the accelerator as she pulled away from him. His criticism stung, but she knew it was inaccurate and unfair. Her regular blogposts pulled in readers from all over the world, who made admiring comments.

Serena could be eloquent when she chose to be, but she had ceased to communicate with Randolph in a civilised manner; she simply couldn't be bothered.

Last Chances

The banks had become tired of waiting for any significant repayment and slapped a re-possession order on the house. Randolph and Serena could have managed the mortgage on its own, but the other loans he had taken out were the problem.

Randolph absolutely refused to sell The Grand Duchess, and kept it insured, but would not do the same for the car that Serena drove herself and the children around in. She protested that this was both illegal and dangerous. 'Drive the Riley then' he would riposte, knowing full well that it was a heavy and difficult car for her to manoeuvre. And she worried that the vintage car gave a completely wrong impression of their financial situation.

Early one morning as Serena and the children sat having breakfast in the little *apartement*, a large blue van and a police car pulled up in the drive. Burly, black-clad men spilt out of the van, and followed a bailiff to the main front door. One of the men started to drill the locks on the front door to force entry.

Hissing at the children to hide all their electrical gadgets in their bedrooms, Serena ran onto the terrace overlooking the drive. She watched, incensed as two men took a battering ram to further open the door. Adrenalin coursing through her veins, and heedless of the danger, she leapt from the balcony to confront them. She knew that she hadn't received prior notice of this invasion, but for all she knew, Randolph might have done so.

Gathering her courage, she stepped forward to halt their entry, complaining about the damage to the front door as they surrounded her intimidatingly. She demanded that they produce identification and a warrant, and when they failed to do so, she raised her phone to photograph the damaged door. One of the thugs promptly knocked it out of her hand, and in doing so caught her on the side of the face. There was a roar of fury from Sebastian watching from above, and he also jumped down onto the drive.

'Did you witness that'? she appealed desperately to the police, but they chose to turn their backs on her, and one of them muttered at her under his breath 'Shut the fuck up'.

However, the bailiff couldn't produce the necessary documentation.

The scene had been witnessed by their immediate neighbours who stood silently in a group and glowered at the police. In that respect everyone stood together, and the intruders departed swiftly.

Afterwards as Serena sat fuming at Randolph's desk, she saw the unopened letter from the bank. It wasn't a warrant for entry, but it was a serious first warning. 'For Christ's sake' she said. It seemed that every day the pressure mounted, and she sank further and further into gloom.

She was fighting this battle alone.

Randolph Goes Missing

Serena couldn't get hold of Randolph to tell him of their plight; she tried for days. He sent Scarlett a brief 'Happy Birthday' text on the appropriate day, but that was the limit of his communication and he went AWOL after that.

For some time, Serena had never known his whereabouts or schedule; he was deliberately vague these days. Whenever she had questioned him, he would fob her off with his 'need to know' speech. He was obsessed with South American politics and the Venezuelan leader Hugo Chávez. When last at home, his television was constantly tuned to the Al-Jazeera news channel and he had spent hours hunched over his laptop ignoring them all.

The attempts Serena had made to confront him about their dire financial situation only resulted in him rounding on her angrily. He told her, through gritted teeth, that her concerns were purely domestic and small-minded, and that she was incapable of seeing the bigger picture – taking a world view. By contrast, he implied, his strictly confidential assignments were so crucially important to international affairs, that the credit he deserved would only come to him posthumously.

Nor had he bothered to erase any history on his computer now. South American dating sites were left open with conversations he had had with scantily dressed pouting ladies. 'It's simply a discreet way for me to send coded messages' he would say. There was always an excuse, always a smokescreen for him to hide behind.

In his cups, he would ramble incoherently about the horrific things he had witnessed. Headless bodies in ditches and armed guards at shop fronts. He also spoke of the worried families who lived behind high walls, with every conceivable alarm and security system to protect them.

'These people live in fear of their lives every moment of every day' he would tell her sombrely and reproachfully, as if her own anxieties were entirely insignificant. Yet Serena wasn't entirely sure that he had been exaggerating. Watching the news, kidnappings of high net worth individuals did seem to be on the increase.

Randolph's office phoned shortly after Scarlett's birthday to say that they too could not get hold of him. Had Serena heard from him herself, she was asked? She said that she hadn't. She was then told that he wasn't contactable at the hotel where he was supposed to be staying but had been seen getting into a car on the previous day. None of the 'hotlines' worked, his mobile phones were unanswered. Was there anything at all she could tell them?

Serena had become friendly with one of the PA's, though Randolph hated this and had coldly told her to keep her distance. But she was past caring, and she did have some news, at least. She asked to speak to her and confided that an email had come through to him on his personal email address. It was from a woman in South America. It was intimate and personal, she said, and not the sort of email a married man should be receiving. It had asked him to fly out somewhere to meet her so that they could connect. If she was a member of the family that he was supposed to be supporting and assisting, then the tone of the letter was inappropriate. Serena had replied and told the woman that he had a family, and to stop writing to him. The PA not unnaturally asked Serena to forward the email.

Sometime later the office phoned back and told her that Randolph was definitely missing from his post and that a replacement was being sent out immediately. Serena's blood ran cold. She imagined him lying dead in some godforsaken spot, wild dogs scavenging off his body. She wouldn't wish that fate on her worst enemy. Randolph's closest friend in France was in his confidence to some degree, so feeling frightened and alone, Serena went to see him. But he gave only cold comfort.

'It's the nature of the job' he said calmly, 'let's hope it was quick for his sake'. Serena sat numbly and drank the wine he offered.

But she didn't have to wait long. The next day the office phoned to tell her that Randolph had eventually been contacted. She was relieved, of course but this was short-lived. He rang her himself, incandescent with rage.

'I told the hotel exactly where I was going' he protested 'and exactly when I would be back. Thanks to your interference I'm now in a very awkward position.'

'But you were missing for days' Serena protested.

'For Christ's sake' he shouted 'I was merely over the border.'

'You're paid to be in Venezuela and contactable, not in Colombia and uncontactable. Or making romantic assignations with some piece of totty' she replied. The phone went dead on her.

Randolph was flown back home and was summoned to explain his conduct. Soon afterwards, his senior took the trouble to phone Serena personally. 'I have to relinquish him' he said, 'I'm very sorry'. Randolph's contract was to be terminated immediately, and as his words sank in, she knew the fight to save their home was lost, thanks to the absolute prat she had married going rogue. She was buggered if she would meet him at the airport.

An angry Randolph ignored Serena for several days after his return, blaming her entirely for the loss of his job. When at last he deigned to speak, he was scathing.

'You just couldn't keep your mouth shut could you', he raged. 'Don't you dare speak to anyone in my office ever again. You have no idea of the damage your meddling has done. You're incredibly and unbelievably dumb. Your jealous and spiteful nature has wrecked my career; you're no better than my ex-wife.' Hardly pausing for breath, he hurled torrent after torrent of abuse at her.

Serena rang the friendly PA, bewildered and close to tears. Surely, she said, any woman in her position – left alone with a family and huge debts – would have reacted as she had? The email was the only clue to Randolph's whereabouts and hadn't she been right to report it? The girl was sympathetic, but Serena couldn't deceive herself. She was married to a man who got a kick from duplicitous behaviour.

Serena thought back to the final season at Le Château. Two of their guests were an undercover policewoman and her psychiatrist friend. They took an immediate dislike to Randolph but invited Serena in for a drink. When asked what he did for a living, Serena was evasive, but clearly miserable. They looked at her with concern.

'Get away from him as fast as you can' they said, 'he's got a borderline personality disorder. Reckless behaviour is typical, and he will drag you down with him'.

Though thinking this a brutal assessment at the time, she now found this to be an accurate analysis of her husband.

She knew she must escape.

The Final Straw

But before it was all over, they were the victims of another dirty trick. Their water consumption had seemed extraordinarily high, but Randolph had been away so much that the problem had not been investigated. Serena vaguely assumed that topping up the pool accounted for the high bills but tried to use as little water as possible in the house. She was always telling Scarlett not to take so long in the shower and she denied herself long soaks in her clawfoot bath.

The farmer they had bought the house from had a spraying machine for his crops, very much like the one Randolph had owned. He kept it in a barn which he hadn't had the sense to sell along with the house. Unwisely joining a co-operative, he now regretted this decision. Although it guaranteed him regular income, he had to come to resent sharing the high prices his own crop had yielded. The barn lay full of rusting and useless pieces of farm machinery that he was too idle to move.

Now that funds were virtually non-existent, and every bill hit them hard, Randolph belatedly began to study them. He waited until the farmer neighbour was cheerfully and noisily filling his sprayer and then strolled out to look at their water meter, pulling off the tight stop cock which had covered it for years. Though the dial was difficult to see beneath a layer of dirt and condensation, it was nevertheless spinning at a crazy rate. He beckoned to Serena, who was watching from the terrace.

'Shit' he said, 'that bastard's water is still connected to our meter, I know exactly how many litres are needed to fill his tank'. Not surprisingly he was right. They both stood glowering at the culprit with their arms folded. He carried on nonchalantly, unaware that Randolph had been a farmer and knew a lot about his machine. When he finished, the dial stopped spinning, and he pulled away towards his fields without a backward glance.

Randolph sat down and calculated how much water had been siphoned over the years based on how many sprayings he would do in a day. The figure ran into thousands of euros. The worst part of it was that they had no definite proof and the new Mayor would not consent to come and view their findings. It would be their word against a family who had lived in the village for generations. The farmer had gone to school with the Mayor. They had probably dated each other's wives, socialised together and watched each other's children grow up. Old friends do not investigate each other willingly. Even so the amount was substantial and the two of them had the irritation of watching him repeatedly fill his tank as the water meter whizzed round.

'No wonder he stands happily for hours at the end of each day washing down his sprayer' Randolph fumed. It was another low blow. But however often they stood and glared at him, he remained unaware that his deceit had been uncovered. In the end Randolph announced that he was definitely going to complain to the Mayor.

'Do we really have to go down this path again'? groaned Serena. 'But this man is stealing from us' Randolph replied. He had a fair point, but she feared they would be simply banging their heads against a brick wall. As expected, the Mayor was annoyed to receive their complaint but had to be seen to be taking it seriously. After a few days a mini digger arrived to try and find the offending pipe. The problem was the digger's owner was from the neighbouring village and almost apologetic to the farmer, whom he knew well.

There was a tense half hour whilst he dug around, just far enough to satisfy Randolph but not far enough to uncover anything. The farmer and his brother looked on anxiously, protesting that the digger was breaching their boundary and they would not let it explore further. The meter stopped going around frantically after that and it came as no surprise to see a new tap fitting which enabled them to get away with their deceit by the skin of their teeth.

Corruption − petty or otherwise − seemed to be so rife in rural France that the price they were paying for living here seemed far too high.

Bizarre Behaviour

Randolph's behaviour after that became more and more bizarre. To a degree, Serena had been attracted by his eccentricity, but his behaviour was now frequently sinister. She came home one day to find him sitting perfectly still with a plastic shopping bag over his head. ill. It was a deeply disturbing sight, but she tried to remain calm and asked him what he was doing. He didn't reply.

Exasperated, she drove to see her friend Lizzy and explained the situation. She rolled her eyes, impatiently, but agreed to accompany Serena back to the Château. Striding into the kitchen, Lizzy asked him briskly what the hell he thought he was doing. He ignored her, but his breathing became more and more laboured as the plastic bag emptied of air.

'For Christ's sake' Lizzy said impatiently, 'you'll suffocate yourself'. She stepped over to the kettle and put it on. 'I'm going to make us all a cup of tea' she said as Serena stood by, anxiously. Randolph carefully removed the bag and smiled smugly at them both. 'A cup of coffee would be marvellous' he drawled. He had obtained the result he required, further upsetting Serena and drawing attention to himself by this ridiculous prank.

On another occasion the satellite dish had become dislodged. The house was three stories high and Randolph had a replacement hip which was giving him trouble. The idea of him clambering over the roof was madness. Even though Serena tearfully begged him not to attempt this, he ignored her and started to climb out of the trap door of the roof.

Serena hared off to the house of a neighbour whose husband was a roofer. He sprinted round immediately and told Randolph not to be so bloody ridiculous. Eventually he persuaded him to climb back down and offered to fix the dish himself. Randolph would later explain his reckless behaviour away by saying that Serena would make his life unbearable if she couldn't watch English television. Her failure to get to grips with the French language was lamentable, he would say, causing her to squirm in embarrassment.

Some days later, Randolph announced that his doctor had given the all clear for another hip replacement. It was entirely his own fault that the first operation hadn't been successful. He had, against all advice, attended a court case only days later. There were numerous steps up to the building. At home later and screaming in agony he had collapsed with the bone poking out at a hideous angle. Serena had dialled 999 and they quickly found themselves on the bumpy rural roads of Dorset.

They filled him with morphine and painkillers, but the journey was still tortuous. 'We should have called the air ambulance' they whispered under their breaths, Randolph gasping with pain. Serena's nerves were in shreds, but Randolph had succumbed to the highs of the drugs. The stretcher was clicked into place and they began to wheel him in. Suddenly it fell to the ground with a sickening thud. Randolph let out an agonised scream and went ashen. The locks hadn't been clicked in correctly. He was quickly hoisted back up without apology and taken into A&E.

After a long wait Serena was led to his ward. Randolph was sitting bolt upright in bed and holding forth in a loud voice.

'Do you know who I am'? he was demanding of the other patients.

'I am the rightful heir to the Romanoff throne; my family were cold bloodedly murdered and hurled to their final resting places like paupers flung into unmarked graves. The bloody royal family of Britain have a lot to answer for, they are just as guilty of murder' he had thundered.

Serena had heard it all before so smiled weakly at the astonished faces.

Now Randolph was insisting on driving himself to hospital in The Grand Duchess. Serena's friend Bella and her boyfriend were over from England, and they collectively urged him not to be so foolish. Arrogant as ever, he wouldn't be dissuaded. Yet when he had driven off, Serena gave a sigh of relief and the three of them spent a relaxed day, picnicking around the pool and reminiscing about old times.

When Serena dutifully phoned to see how the operation had gone, Randolph reported that all was well. He had opted for a local anaesthetic, preferring to be awake for the whole procedure, all the better to repeat all the gory details later. Helping the gardening-mad Bella to collect seeds from the poppies in the garden, Serena was just beginning to think she might have a few days peace when the unmistakeable sound of The Grand Duchess tore through the early evening silence of the village. As the elegant car made its entrance, a gleeful Randolph clutching the wheel just like Mr Toad, they shook their heads in disbelief. He had discharged himself from hospital.

'Is he *completely* insane?' asked a shocked Bella.

Serena merely shrugged. By now, she *knew* that he was. It had occasionally crossed her mind that she herself might be going bonkers, but no one had yet hinted this. Yet she had made some idiotic and careless decisions, without realising the consequences.

Randolph slowly heaved himself out of the car grimacing with pain. 'And has the hospital given you permission to leave'? Serena asked him icily.

'No' he boasted. 'I have made my own very daring escape'.

'Very heroic I'm sure' she said sarcastically, as Bella prodded her astonished boyfriend into lounging forward to lend Randolph a supportive arm.

It was a balmy warm evening the air heavy with the fragrance of the countryside. Its sweetness and the presence of her sympathetic yet watchful friends lulled Serena into a false sense of security. Bats swooped and squealed in the twilight, flashes of black against the deepening darkness of the sky. They lay back in chairs and star-gazed whilst Randolph recounted the story of his latest escape.

The Destruction of a Beautiful Village

It wasn't long before the hum of the diggers could be heard as they began to tear out the heart of the neighbouring field, uprooting all the vines and wild flowers. An ancient brick wall which supported a rusting cross was knocked down in a morning. (It eventually reappeared in a new wall built by a man who had been paid compensation for the loss of a slight strip of land). Certain villagers began to appear in new four-wheel drive cars. The wife would perch grandly beside her husband as they drove to the local supermarket looking smug and pleased with themselves. Serena was disgusted by this further evidence of skulduggery.

Other things were conspiring to make her miserable. Their beloved dog had developed an ear infection and the cost of the vet's bills had become prohibitive. Randolph was still refusing to sell the Grand Duchess, maintaining that Basil was Serena's responsibility. Accompanied by Sebastian, she took him for yet another examination and was told his quality of life was no longer good. They went outside to confer and came to the sad conclusion that it was kinder to put him to sleep. They both cried all the way home, and for days afterwards would find tears in their eyes at the loss of such a loyal pet. Randolph merely snorted that Serena's ability to care for any animal was lamentable. She went into the garage and kicked the Grand Duchess angrily.

Not long afterwards, Sebastian moved to a little flat in Carcassonne. He was now eighteen and told Serena that he needed to live his own life, away from the drama and madness that swirled around Randolph. Serena felt bereft, as she supposed any mother did when their first born fled the nest. Hanging washing out in the garden, she would recall similar afternoons when Sebastian had come swinging round the corner, home from college with his rucksack on his back. The hollyhocks were just finishing and lolling against the long-whitewashed wall. Wild sweet strawberries hung in profusion over a low wall and the grasses were encouraged to mingle with poppies and other wild flowers. All should have been bliss in the garden of Eden, but Serena felt empty. She now hated the vastness of the giant house looming over her. She wanted her boy back home whatever the problems.

She went up to his room and buried her face in his pillow, hoping for a trace of his familiar smell. A few forlorn mismatched socks lay on the floor. She automatically picked them up for the wash. She placed his teddy lovingly on his bed and adjusted the figure of a footballer, hanging from a metal frame. She felt overwhelmingly lonely and knew that all her dreams had died.

The banks were now constantly harassing them. If they failed to make the payments demanded they would foreclose and sell off the house for a pittance to recover their costs. As usual Serena was the one attempting to stave off the inevitable. Randolph simply ranted, drank and railed against his fate. She put Le Château up for sale on the internet, using her beautiful photographs and a succinct but tempting description of its amenities. A potential buyer flew over from England for the weekend. He put forward a very reasonable verbal offer and suggested they crack open a bottle of champagne.

Serena found the effort of pretending that everything was normal so stressful that after two glasses she felt faint. She excused herself and went and threw up in the loo. When she returned her face was ashen. A very refreshed Randolph chortled 'Ah, here's my talented wife, you'll have to excuse her — she can't hold her drink'. She could quite happily have punched him, but instead was forced to smile placatingly and claim that something she had eaten earlier had disagreed with her.

Please Sign

Serena started to scour the papers for somewhere suitable to live. The purchaser of Le Château was driving a hard bargain and time was not on her side. Their equity was fast diminishing as the interest on the original loan kept increasing and their other debts grew. It was going to be a case of downsizing yet finding a property that could still earn its keep. Randolph was hugely disgruntled and grumbled that they should be looking to rent, not buy.

Serena ignored him. She was determined to buy again, needing that security when everything else in her life was uncertain. There was one – far smaller – property in their price range which she thought she could turn into a pleasing rental business. Praying that their sale would go through, she put in an offer, which was accepted. But the timings were incredibly tight.

They began the onerous business of packing up. It simply wasn't possible to take everything, so trailer loads of their furniture passed through the village on the way to the *déchetterie*. Neighbours who had taken Jean-Claude's backhanders stopped and helped themselves.

The house was utter chaos. 'Randolph, do throw out some of your crap' Serena begged as the exchange date loomed closer.

'As a man of intellect, I need my reference books around me at all times, which you are incapable of understanding' he would simply intone, reaching for the gut-rotting plonk which he insisted on drinking, night after night. He refused to go through any of his boxes of paperwork, file upon file of litigation going back years. They were including an awful lot of furniture in the sale so that the new owners could also run a rental business. Serena would look at pictures of the house years later and find that they were still using her images.

With only forty-eight hours to go before the banks had the right to foreclose, they drove over to the notaries to formalise the sale. Serena had doubled the dose of her anti-stress tablets that morning. They arrived in good time but were deftly ushered to a side-room by a rather dandyish *notaire*. He was looking worried.

'We appear to have a slight problem' he murmured.

'What sort of a problem'? enquired Serena apprehensively.

'The buyer's wife doesn't want to sign the papers' he told them. He shifted his highly polished shoes from foot to foot. A feeling of *déjà vu* swept over Serena; Luke had lost their London home in a dreadfully similar situation. Surely this couldn't be happening to her again? The *notaire* smiled and said they should step inside his office. Their buyer was looking on helplessly as his much younger second wife paced up and down the room furiously whilst trying to pacify a baby. The pair was hissing insults at each other, and it was clear that he was putty in her hands.

Serena said nothing but sat down quietly, discreetly popping another calming tablet into her mouth. She had begun to float a little by this time and was trying to raise herself above it all by pretending it wasn't happening. The buyer's wife then proceeded to denigrate every aspect of Serena's beautiful home. She forced herself to look away and dug her nails into her palms, to stop herself from giving this harpy a tongue lashing that she wouldn't forget in a hurry. Having run out of invective, the woman held the pen crossly over the piece of paper lingering for what seemed an eternity.

Serena popped another tablet, vaguely wondering if she was risking an overdose. But perhaps it was the lesser of two evils; she suspected she would have a heart attack if this all went horribly wrong. But the fight had not entirely gone out of her. The couple had already had their furniture delivered to Le Château and it was stacked in two of the downstairs room. Serena rose to her feet.

'It's entirely up to you whether you sign or not' Serena stated 'but as all your furniture and possessions are in my property, I have every right to dispose of it all. I might even have a bonfire. If you choose not to sign, you will have just four hours to remove it'. She sat down again and folded her arms.

'Just sign the fucking paper' the husband hissed, well aware that hiring another van at short notice would prove difficult if not impossible. And although she glared at Serena, his wife signed. Serena thought she might faint with relief.

'Well' said Randolph pompously, 'what extraordinary behaviour'.

Carcassonne Beckons

Next, they had to sign the papers for the new home that Serena had found in central Carcassonne. It was an *apartement* in a Maison de Maître of historical interest, dating back to 1720. It wasn't anywhere near as majestic as the château, but its layout made it suitable for running as a *chambre d'hôte* as their living accommodation could be made separate from the guest rooms. The only reservation Serena had was that most of the building was owned by a female *notaire* who used one *apartement* as her office, and she sensed hostile vibes from her when they arrived for the signing.

The building itself was imposing with enormous double wooden front doors. Serena imagined horse-drawn carriages sweeping through them into the courtyard beyond. Inside a wide stone staircase led to the upper floors. Serena had been told by the agent that they would have shared access to the common parts. 'But do we have access to the garden'? she asked. This time it was her pen poised above the paper. The agent looked uneasy and shot a glance towards the elderly owner. Yet it was the unsmiling *notaire* who answered, with an abrupt 'Non' although why she was there, since she wasn't acting for the seller, was unclear.

The house had been in the same family for over three generations and gradually been divided up for them, but over the years *apartement* after *apartement* had been acquired by the *notaire*. Their seller, a sprightly ninety-year-old was accompanied by his much younger sixth wife. Presumably she wasn't keen to live alongside the ghosts of his family or his previous five wives. The building also held unhappy wartime memories. The old man's brother had been identified as a collaborator and one morning he and other traitors were rounded up and shot, up against the ancient walls of the fortified town. He was never spoken of again.

Serena was to learn, too late, that there was no love lost between the *notaire's* father and the elderly gentleman and he had refused to sell to her. It turned out that she had already acquired – and closed off – the garden where the only brother now living in the building had played as a boy. It was a spiteful act as she herself lived in a large property nearby, with an enormous garden and pool. Now he was slipping into the twilight world of dementia. Serena would find him wandering up and down the stone staircase in slippers and dressing gown completely bewildered.

Serena knew that she would miss having a garden and something didn't feel quite right about this transaction. But Randolph was becoming impatient and convinced as ever of his own superior knowledge of the law., and he urged her to sign. It wasn't long before it became clear that the *notaire* strongly resented the fact that the *apartement* had not fallen into their hands for a song.

The Affair Breaks

Randolph soon became bored and restless. He found running a bed and breakfast in a very different environment to Le Château beneath his dignity. Serving up *croissants* every morning just wasn't his style; he deemed it far too menial, and with the medieval city on their doorstep their guests were not much inclined to listen to his stories. He could no longer play *le grand seigneur*.

A lively young friend of theirs called Suzy dropped by one morning after working in an all-night café. She egged Randolph on to join her for a breakfast drink, and this quickly became a daily occurrence. Serena didn't much care; she had lost patience with him and it was actually a relief that someone was taking him off her hands for an hour or two. She was busy putting all her energies into promoting the business online to keep them afloat, seeing Sebastian as often as she could and helping Scarlett with her schoolwork.

Because of the age difference between Randolph and Suzy the thought that their friendship might be developing into an affair didn't occur to her. Serena would have been the first to admit that she had become rather rounded and cosy recently, but Randolph's acid comments about her figure did not spur her to try and lose the extra weight. Not that Randolph was any kind of Adonis. She did sometimes wonder if they were looking in the same mirror because he viewed himself in the best possible light, despite his thinning hair and drink-stained teeth. She retreated more and more into her own private world.

It hurt Randolph's pride that Serena was again building a successful business out of nothing. Resentment turned to malice, and he set out to seduce Suzy, who was only too willing to be seduced. From a relatively humble background, she had fallen for his aristocratic act. Yet this affair was so entirely lacking the panache of his previous dalliances, that Serena was simply amazed when she caught them out. It all seemed terribly sordid. Serena imagined that a fling with a friend's husband would feel spicier than an affair *per se* and thrillingly illicit.

When Serena confronted Randolph with firm evidence of his straying, he was watching his favourite tv soap. He had looked up, an expression of boredom mixed with irritation on his face.

'I really can't think what you're complaining about' he said languidly. 'After all, it takes the strain off *you*'.

Serena gasped. An affair was just what the wine-swilling selfish bastard thought he needed; it was a pathetic attempt to relive his glory days. Serena felt that she now understood his first wife perfectly and in less than thirty seconds informed him sternly that their marriage was over.

***

The fallout from their separation was nasty and bitter, just as it had been with his previous wife. Randolph moved in with Suzy, but word soon reached Serena that their physical affair had ended as soon as their cover was blown. This did not prevent a vengeful Randolph from accusing Serena of all sorts of bad behaviour, and Suzy openly derided her on social media. Randolph never spoke to Scarlett and Sebastian again, brushing past them in the street as though they did not exist, colder than stone itself.

Anxious to protect Scarlett from this ugly situation Serena took the excruciating decision to send her back to England. Some former guests had offered her a job in their family business. But she missed her daughter terribly and longed for her company. For weeks afterwards, she put off removing Scarlett's personal things from the bathroom cupboard, almost if she expected her to bounce through the door. When she nerved herself to do so, it took ages, as she found herself sniffing every perfume spray and bottle of lotion in the hope of briefly bringing her daughter closer, gulping back tears.

Randolph spent hours composing subtle yet cruel letters which would have broken most people, but Serena would not descend to his level. He took to stalking her through the city and waiting until the front door was open, would sit in the dark cellar of the building, refusing to move until he got tired or wanted a drink. Sometimes he and Suzy would deliberately drive past the house screaming obscenities as they took their boot full of empty bottles to be recycled. He would tell people that Serena had been placed in rehab, and worst of all, he wrote obscene and disgusting letters to her parents.

Serena had seen it all before. 'No fool like an old fool' was one of Randolph's favourite sayings. Somewhere in that befuddled head of his he must, she thought, be aware that he had made a laughing-stock of himself by being caught with his trousers down.

An old fool indeed.

No.18, Warwickshire

Serena sat contemplating her post-Randolph life on her plush English feather-filled sofa. The style wasn't quite what she had envisaged for her now chic French *apartement* when perusing it lovingly online, but it complemented her French antique pieces well enough. The ornate gold-embossed mirror above her grey marble fireplace afforded her a direct and not entirely pleasing reflection of herself.

'I am fifty-five' she thought, 'my second marriage is over, and late middle-age is upon me'.

Her life danced and flirted alongside the flames of the fire and taunted her from a distance she could not reach. 'I am fast approaching my twilight years' she reflected, and she heard the voice of her mother Evelyn forty years earlier.

She could see her now, in a close-fitting dark blue lace dress accessorised by sheer navy-blue stockings and indecently high heels. 'Life goes by frighteningly fast darling, suddenly before you know it, you'll be the age I am now'. Serena hear the cruel echo of her own similar words to her daughter Scarlett. Her daughter had stared at her incredulously.

'Don't be so morbid mother, I'll never be as old as you anyway' and she recalled the raucous, although not unkind laughter that followed. Serena too had naively thought it would never be possible, nor had she imagined hereditary traits revealing themselves as the years passed by. Even the same subdued paint colours of her drawing-room echoed those favoured by Evelyn. She had silently, and without realising it morphed into her mother, the woman whose stylish attire and innate sense of elegance had irritated the hell out of her when she was younger. How she had resented her ability to turn heads when she entered a room.

Looking back, she remembered her childhood home exactly as it had stood when her parents had taken her and her twin brother to view it for the first time. A slippery and very steep path with towering flowers and weeds tumbling down the low walls led to the house. The entrance had seemed rather secretive and mysterious. An elderly but clearly refined lady had opened the handsome front door at the top of stone steps, containing a metal boot scraper which had fascinated the excited children.

The inside of the house enchanted her immediately. Dark wooden floorboards gave off the unmistakable odour of beeswax whilst faded thin rugs clung onto their diminishing glory in the centre of every room. A wide panelled fire surround with diamond shaped glass doors held a large collection of delicate pale pink and blue figurines. In the grate, a meagre fire lay flickering and piles of dogeared books lay scattered on every small table, threatening to break their delicate legs. The house was large and felt uncomfortably cold. It took Serena a while to realise there were no bright white radiators on the walls unlike their present home.

They all trooped silently into the kitchen where there was an ancient metal range. Huge flat hot plates held a jumble of tired looking saucepans all jostling hopelessly for space. Underneath the range a fire burnt steadily giving Serena the impression she was visiting an exhibition in a museum. Above the door a line of sturdy bells clearly marked with each room sat solemnly silent.

·'I'm afraid only the master bedroom and the dining room still have working bells to call for service'. The clipped tones of the elderly lady hung on the air as she surveyed the family before her who would eventually call her lifelong home theirs. Reverently, following her up the wide staircase their footsteps echoed despite the thin runner held precariously in place by the brass stair rods. A small landing halfway up contained a glorious stained-glass window from which you could enjoy the view whilst comfortably seated on the quaint window seat.

'I would sit here as a child' the lady said, 'and watch the steam trains go by, counting the cows and sheep dotted on the hills beyond. It's all rather different now' she added wistfully. Serena turned and followed her gaze. She could indeed see the railway track but instead of the romantic and gentle view of contented animals there loomed the ugly new Council offices. Beyond that was the spire of the church and solid looking red brick houses surrounded by thick coniferous hedging marking out their territory. The lady, Serena later learnt, was called Miss Smith, an ordinary name for the obviously not-very-ordinary lady before her. She led them silently into the various bedrooms that led off the main landing. Another nugget of information that Serena gleaned was the fact that Miss Smith was a spinster. Her mother explained what this meant, and Serena thought it sounded sad. Spinsters were ladies who never married or had children so that when they became elderly and infirm, they had no-one to love and care for them.

Yet Miss Smith had produced a book which became a publishing phenomenon. Serena would eventually attribute this partly to the freedom of not being responsible for anyone else. Later Evelyn took great pride in informing visitors that it was the very spot which had led to the penning of *Country Diaries*. She would add the last snippet of information with a flourish lest any of them failed to appreciate the literary legacy of the house. Miss Smith's lovely illustrations of Warwickshire's country lanes and wild life made an innocuous and acceptable gift for ladies of a certain age. Serena admired the talent and diligence of this Edwardian lady who had found the stamina to bicycle round the country, pursuing and recording her genteel passion.

Another part of the house, fascinating to the twins, was reached by a second narrow staircase. Originally the servant's quarters with a mean, small fireplace it nevertheless gave an uninterrupted view of the parkland behind. It resembled a poet's garret and indeed Serena later wrote her very first poem entitled 'Heaven's Pearly Gates'. Slowly and painfully tapped out on her mother's old typewriter, the ribbon worn and thin from use but never replaced, she had hung onto the original copy. In the intervening years she had constantly berated herself for not making time to write more, as she loved to do. But she hadn't, because life had moved swiftly on, just as her Mother had forewarned her it would.

No.11 Carcassonne

With the worrying thought in her mind that the sins of her youth might actually exclude her from the Pearly gates of heaven, as depicted in her poem, Serena was jolted back to the present. She noticed with some alarm that her neck was beginning to wrinkle. Stretching it upwards slightly, her image in the mirror softened by the evening light as it gently started to envelop the city, she glanced over at the clock on the mantelpiece. It resolutely stated half past five; another thirty minutes to go before she could decently pour a much-needed drink. Recently her friend Abbey had taken to visiting and slyly putting the clock forward by twenty minutes so that they could convince themselves they weren't verging on alcoholism.

Her business was going well, and she had plenty of glowing internet reviews. This amused her. It wasn't that the routine bored her, but rather that once she had met the challenge of a new venture, she found herself distracted and looking for new horizons. This morning she had been rather offhand with a guest who had complained about a triviality. Now she longed for a glass of cooling rosé from the bottle she had carefully selected earlier on. It had been a frustrating day overall and now her current guests were knocking on her door, wanting fresh glasses and ice cubes for their aperitifs.

Whilst she was serving them, she fed them titbits of information about the area, which she had researched carefully. It was easy to view Carcassonne as a tourist trap, but she liked to guide her visitors off the beaten track. The more sociable of the guests would join her for a glass of wine and they would exchange life stories of travels and more. She would never say that her life was boring *per se* but the inevitability of it all sometimes felt like a heavy blanket draped over her.

Earlier that day the garage had telephoned her to inform her that her beloved VW Golf convertible which had been towed away after breaking down for the umpteenth time was dead.

'Vraiment, elle est mort' the man had shouted at her as she feigned disbelief, a note of triumph in his voice that he had successfully conveyed the news to her.

'Okay' Serena had mumbled unhappily, 'Okay' being a universal way to terminate a conversation. As Abbey hadn't yet appeared her thoughts turned to sampling some of the home-grown hashish she had been entrusted with. She had just taken a tentative puff when the phone rang shrilly, and she felt compelled to answer it immediately. The voice of her boisterous cousin boomed at her, jangling her nerves. Being both male and half-French, she knew that his dealings with the garage would be far more productive and had asked him to challenge the car's death sentence. It had been a mistake to indulge in the ill-rolled joint because she began to feel hazy and disorientated as he continued his conversation.

'The man from the garage says because it's a classic car it's worth opening up the engine'. He waited for her response.

'How much'? Serena asked fearfully. The figure he quoted was prohibitive as she knew it would be.

'He says they are collectable' he added as though this would soften the blow. Serena paused letting out a tired sigh.

'Sleep on it' he suggested, knowing a replacement was totally out of the question.

'Yes, I will, thanks' she agreed, placing the phone back in its little cradle and finally feeling slightly pacified by the effects of the spliff.

She awoke the next day but felt slightly fuzzy for no reason. Her left leg had been painful for a couple of weeks and she had felt both numbness and tingling in her left arm. She had pushed it from her mind, thinking that she sat too long at the computer on an unsuitable chair. She was permanently tired these days. Accepting the fact that age was finally creeping up on her, she hadn't noticed another stealthy shadow inching slowly closer, waiting to envelop her in darkness. Breathing out deeply, she wondered for the umpteenth time how things had come to this point. She had never in her life lived like this, forced to sleep in the attic alongside a portable loo so that the full letting potential of the apartment could be realised. To reach her 'bedroom' she had to climb up some precarious metal step ladders and crawl through a tiny hole roughly sawn through the ancient beams in the ceiling. Once she had clambered her way up there however the large new Velux window at least let in some light. If she placed some worn and paint splattered wooden step ladders carefully underneath it, she could climb up and survey the rooftops of the city and the mountains beyond.

At night she would cautiously creep up with the knowledge that the window prevented her from the sheer drop to the garden below. She would look at the stars and silently laugh to herself that she could survey her rooftop world undisturbed and unseen. When she had first dragged her camp bed up there, she would lie rigid, imagining rats scurrying over the rooftops in search of food, terrified that they would linger by her open window and slink down and crawl over her bed.

Such was her fear that she scrupulously combed the dusty floorboards for crumbs or signs of vermin droppings. Once she had convinced herself that the rats weren't interested in visiting her attic, she began to worry that the rooftop cats would find her and seek comfort from her warm slumbering body. She dreaded waking to find a ghastly fat stray animal with matted, stinking fur lying contently beside her. But neither of these nightmares materialized and she began to enjoy the anonymity of her den.

She had to make the best of her situation; if she looked at it too closely, she might sink into despair. Once she had taken a photograph as she lay back on her bed and when she looked at it afterwards, she was shocked by the starkness and the reality of the image. The old damp dark brown stains of years of leakage through the roof and the holes where the plasterwork had given up added to her anxiety. Sometimes when she went to bed, she would brush away the tiny bits of hard plaster that had fallen on her sheets.

'What a bloody existence' she would think and then silently berate herself running mental pictures through her head of people far less fortunate. She knew there were many and she would resolutely inform her mother that she was fine.

'I have a roof over my head, so I'm dry.'

'I have sufficient food in front of me.'

'I have the support of my family and those I love'.

No-one needed any-more did they? She would argue with herself that she had no right to expect or demand more although sometimes a little voice in her head whined that a little more would not go amiss. She desperately tried not to think of the people she knew who had so much more, the people who openly shot her looks of pity as they went up to her attic on the pretext of 'looking around'. Why they did so Serena would never understand but the humiliation burnt silently and furiously within her.

One woman had remarked what good taste she had, whilst admiring a few old artefacts which lay casually around the *apartement,* but Serena knew that what she really meant was 'How can you live like this?' as she gave her a long thoughtful look of concern. This made Serena want to shout and scream and make an ungodly spectacle of herself. Perhaps, on reflection she should have done…things were certainly stressful enough to justify an outburst.

The roof of her *apartement* was being totally replaced making it necessary to have scaffolding outside the whole of the building. Rather awkwardly some of the shutters were unable to be opened leading to complaints from her guests who were paying rather a lot of money to stay there. It was happening at the very worst time too; at the height of the summer season and she certainly couldn't afford to close. The constant thumping and banging was far louder and more disruptive than she had imagined. She was constantly in a state of anxiety that her guests would walk out, asking for a refund.

She did receive one stinging review from an individual that she'd gone the extra mile for. The ones with serious money were the worst, expecting everything to be just perfect for them. She could picture the pinched anxious face of the wife hovering round her sour-faced husband. Their bedroom was an elegant, calm and spacious room with original flooring and a working open fireplace. A tall sturdy wooden *armoire* towered over the ornate wrought iron bed. It wasn't possible to install air conditioning because the house was a listed building. This vital fact bypassed many. Complaints of lack of double glazing and a lift were common especially amongst the Americans. She was frankly heartily sick of pandering to these people with no imagination or sense of history.

The replacement of the roof was brutal. She had never imagined that the entire *apartement* would shudder as they forcibly wrenched off the old wooden panelling from the thick and ancient beams, the nails screaming as they were removed from their home of centuries. She had to admit that the roofers were a jolly bunch though. They would wave cheerfully as they went past the windows despite the desperately hot temperatures outside. Serena found herself striving to expand her tolerance levels. She would take deep breaths and try to lower herself subconsciously into a calm place, reminding herself that one day it would all simply cease to matter.

But sometimes she did feel overwhelmed. She had once gone up into the attic to be confronted by the expanse of blue sky above viewed through a huge ugly black gaping hole. Two of the men stood grinning at her in an unconcerned manner as they stood in 'her bedroom'. The dust swirled around them and quickly found its way up her nostrils.

'For fuck's sake' she said, between sneezes

'For fuck's sake' they repeated and laughed, pleased with themselves for repeating her English swearing. She couldn't be cross with them, it wasn't their fault the roof was in such an appalling state. She would take them buckets of ice to cool them down and they would shuffle their feet in an embarrassed fashion. They weren't used to small kindnesses, certainly not from the miserable *notaire* in the office downstairs who spoke to no-one. Serena referred to her as the 'sour faced puss'.

Serena was a thorn in the woman's side, as she had unwittingly thwarted her plans. If she had followed her instincts and made discreet enquiries beforehand, she would have been advised that to avoid inevitable conflict she should avoid purchasing the *apartement*. Randolph had put paid to that by insisting that they go ahead. The *notaire* was using her legal knowledge and position to make constant difficulties. It wasn't clear cut corruption, she was far too clever and cunning for that, but rather an insidious drip-feed of difficulties and red-tape. The agents who administered the building just simpered and grovelled to the bitch. There were always heaps of endless paperwork piled high on her table, relating to yet another petty complaint from her neighbour. Serena had belatedly discovered that there wasn't anyone in the town who had a good word to say about her, but she was feared, and no one had spoken out. Unmarried and apparently unsought, she was coldly meticulous in her quest to bring Serena to her knees.

The most uplifting part of Serena's day was her early morning cycle ride to the *boulangerie*. People would wave from the cafés and restaurants as they set up for the day. When she rode up to the sombre dark green front door of the house the workmen would chorus 'Bonjour Madame' and smile as she applied her screeching brakes. Every day she wondered why she hadn't bothered to apply oil to the bike and why she hadn't accepted the baker's offer to cut the spindly *baguette* in half. Every morning it would swing precariously out of the flimsy bag hanging off her shoulder.

That morning the cakes she had bought for her guests were

particularly soft and rounded like comfortable bosoms with a sprinkling of coconut and a cherry on top. Surely the baker must see the resemblance? Perhaps it was to cheer up the thin anxious women with greying hair and worried faces clutching onto their worn wicker baskets. Every day the routine was the same as they scuttled round the shops early to beat the tourists and the heat.

Serena liked to imagine them arriving home. 'Pour toi, mon cheri' they might say, and an elderly husband's eyes would light up as his gaze took in the sight of the proffered treat. Would he make a saucy remark or suggestion she wondered, and hoped that when she finally attained a similar age, she would be living with a man who could?

'Vous êtes sportif!' the roofers shouted encouragingly as her bike slid to a halt that morning. Not *sportif* enough thought Serena gloomily, to give her the glorious toned thighs that she desired. But later that morning, vanity was pushed aside as the pain in her leg started to increase to a worrying level. For the umpteenth time she Googled 'signs of a stroke', eventually picking up the phone and forcing herself to request, as firmly as possible, an appointment with her doctor that evening. Once the time had been set, she felt marginally better and flicked through her diary again checking the arrival time of the guests she expected that day.

But then she felt an overwhelming desire to lie down and give her legs a rest. The air suddenly seemed too stifling and she felt light headed as the room began to swim alarmingly. She managed to elevate her leg on a lumpy feather cushion, so that if felt less painful. She sent a text message to Sebastian who lived close by.

'I feel rather odd' it said; nothing too sensational just to the point. She didn't have anyone else to tell and thought she ought to.

'What do you mean'? he replied instantly, but she couldn't explain because an odd popping had started in her head. When she tried to describe it afterwards it was like the sound of rice-krispies as they crackled in a bowl of milk. She tried to remain calm and take stock of where she was, but alarm bells had started to sound in her head. She texted Sebastian again.

'Call an ambulance now Mum' he replied. She dialled the required number and then felt oddly fraudulent, as though she had no right to be unwell. She couldn't remember her address clearly nor imagine how they would gain entry. The *notaire* had refused a simple entry button, which meant she had to run down and open the huge outer door to all visitors. Fortunately for Serena this morning one of *la notaire's* clients had unwittingly left it open.

L'Hôpital Part Two

Serena staggered to her feet and tried to focus on her predicament. She was now resigned to being carted off to hospital. Automatically she placed the necessary medical card and her mobile in her bag and glanced out of the window. Still no sign of an ambulance. She couldn't remember what she had said, it was a complete blank to her as the fuzziness in her head continued and her body started to float dreamily. Was she in the middle of a heart attack, a stroke, or a complete mental breakdown? Yet part of her was beyond caring; she simply wanted rest and peace.

Finally, the ambulance crew arrived alongside Sebastian who had sprinted over, his handsome young face etched with concern as he stood over her. Her blood pressure was taken whilst they spoke rapidly amongst themselves. She wondered if she had been over dramatic, perhaps she should have tried the deep breathing again, and remained lying down. Once it was ascertained that she was a full-time resident in France, and that the required paperwork was in order she was helped down the wide central stone stairway that served the whole house. As she did so she felt her problems float away from her and lie discarded on those ancient dusty steps.

None of her neighbours were visible for which she was grateful. She was still wearing the garish yellow t-shirt which had only a few hours previously elicited a whistle of admiration as she had cycled to the *boulangerie*. Carcassonne was hosting the start of the *Tour de France*. A damp squib if ever there was one, she had thought at the time. Hours of pre-race excitement, car salesmen bellowing into microphones, men dressed up as clowns and people holding up their phones excitedly ready to catch the action as it whizzed by. It all seemed a lot of fuss over nothing very much – or maybe that was a reflection of how she was feeling about life in general. An awful lot of effort for very little return.

Arriving at the hospital she was placed in a small room in the accident and emergency department. Other people looking seriously depressed at the long wait for treatment stared morosely at their feet whilst grossly overweight women in clingy lurid clothing gesticulated irritably into their mobile phones to which they appeared to be attached. Serena found herself lying next to an elderly woman who was gently moaning and attached to a heart monitor. Her phone kept 'pinging' informing her of incoming messages which she ignored. She took a 'selfie' and then had the disturbing thought that should she die the very last image of her would be grotesque.

'Your mother was one sick woman' the doctors would tell her children and shake their heads sadly. Her own mother would be horrified that she could contemplate such a thing without applying lipstick, yet Serena felt too exhausted to care – or delete the image. She supposed that in the great scheme of life itself her current mental state would be deemed unstable. 'Years of drug abuse' Randolph would have sneered, as if a few clumsily rolled joints constituted a serious drug problem.

Her friends and children had gathered round, stroking her hand and cradling her head whilst telling her they loved her. Her mother had emailed that it was just 'one more hurdle' in her life and that she would overcome it because she was ultimately strong. Serena wasn't sure any more, her confidence in her essential resilience had been sorely knocked, but she allowed herself to gently drift into unconsciousness.

Life Moves On

Serena woke early and rolling out of bed, she moved to the window and watched the sun rise over the gently rolling Dorset hills. The day ahead of her was full of promise. She was spending her convalescence back in England whilst Sebastian kept an eye on her business.

It was wonderful to hear the screeching of the seagulls circling overhead outside instead of listening out warily for the scratchings of unseen mice or loud thumps on the front door. She was free of the hidden terrors and the bullying that her last days in France had entailed. Instead of endless rows of vines on the horizon there were trees and bright shiny little cars. She felt that she was finally managing to steer her life along an even path.

Had anyone asked her if she was happy, she would have replied 'Well I'm not *unhappy*'. She was taking pleasure in small things. If her thoughts ever threatened to unbalance her, at least here she had a stunning coastline to walk along, bordered by fields of cows grazing contentedly. She could climb a hill covered in sweet gorse and fill her lungs with the bracing air of the ocean. There was a favourite spot of hers where she could rest. If she inclined her head slightly, she could view the seemingly endless stretch of coast, curving in the distance. She would murmur out loud how lucky she was, but occasionally she was conscious of a yearning for Carcassonne's narrow streets, and its elegant tall buildings. As she grew stronger in mind and body, she knew she had put enough distance between herself and her past, so it was with excitement that she planned a trip back to France.

When she stepped off the plane at the tiny airport the familiar wall of dry heat hit her immediately. Seen from the air the lush green of England was replaced by the regimented rows of vines and parched soil. Dots of bright blue or turquoise signalled that the climate here was so different as to warrant an outdoor pool. Down in southern France it was the norm rather than a sign of an opulent lifestyle. Her clothing, especially her shoes, already felt cumbersome and heavy. Her fellow travellers all looked wan and pale as they walked towards the waiting locals. Although they looked similar the two groups were poles apart in culture and tradition. Serena felt the familiar tightening of her chest and a constriction in the back of her throat as an indescribable sadness threatened to engulf her. It was understandable, though. Her family were now torn between two countries and this was hard to come to terms with, though she did try. 'The past is the past' she would think, 'I can't change it, I can't go back and do things differently, so I must enjoy the present and look to the future'.

Serena had realised too late that she had put her energies into people and projects that gave her nothing in return, and sometimes she still worried that she had a poor sense of judgement. She hated it when this little bubble of doubt rose to the surface and the familiar feeling of having let the people down that she most loved harangued and plagued her. She chewed on the inside of her lip to stop the tears falling and blinked rapidly as the increasingly unfamiliar bright sunlight confronted her outside the airport. She hadn't asked anyone to meet her and shuffling along with the tourists, she flung her small bag onto a seat in the airport bus.

Worried looking couples kept anxiously together yet despite the driver speaking English and re-assuring everybody that they would be dropped off at their destinations some people still insisted on loudly stating where they wanted to go. She double checked her bag again to make sure the bulky keys to her *apartement* were safely there. She took out a soft chewy mint and looked out of the window. The ride to the centre of the city was dreary and she thought that had she been a tourist she would have felt deflated at the sight of the cheaply built housing estates with their minute little boxes painted in pink and beige. They were edged with shiny evergreens and on the drives were garish cars with metallic folding sunscreens in the front windows.

As they passed the familiar out of town supermarkets Serena was instantly transported back to the many occasions when she had pulled up outside them and sauntered up and down the aisles, filling her trolley with anything that took her fancy. They felt so different to English supermarkets — the smell was stronger for one thing — but the displays also drew you to them with their fascinating array of choices. Cheeses would be on tiny beds of straw separated by plastic parsley whilst the salads would sit looking fresh and enticing, blasted by icy cold steam. The curly leaves looked like bright green frilly knickers with thousands of droplets of water, almost an art form in themselves and much prettier than a crisp Cos lettuce.

A slight chill would indicate that the fresh fish counter was close by piled high with mountains of ice, the floor tiles ridged so that the water from the melting blocks wouldn't sit in puddles on the floor. She would feast her eyes on heaps of slippery pink prawns nestling amongst glistening halves of lemon, and flat bony fish with spiky scales and minute eyes, or large fat bulbous fish with gaping mouths and glazed eyes. The fishmonger would be wearing wellington boots with a waterproof apron and possess red hands, raw from handling all the icy dead bodies. Serena would pause and purchase a large bag of glistening *moules* their deep black shells clacking noisily against each other.

Next, she would slip inside her basket a rounded bulb of purple tinged garlic, a tub of *crème fraiche* and two bottles of white wine; a cheap one for cooking and a delicate, dry one to enjoy with her supper. A matured soft cheese would serve as her dessert, with perhaps some fresh figs too, depending on the season.

The cheery driver indicated that hers was the next stop. A large square surrounded by imposing houses had been deconstructed to make way for an underground car park which never seemed to be full so how necessary it had been was debatable. It was a great shame really that inelegant monstrosities had been allowed to mushroom before the French woke up to their heritage and realized it was what the tourists expected and desired. The vast expanse of concrete was already cracked and uneven and the thin strips of grass patchy and adorned with small piles of dog mess. The most striking building on the square was a bank with curved pillars and ornate stonework. Decorative tiles depicting angels holding garlands hovered over the front entrance. Once a grand town house with views over the park, it now had double-glazed windows with harsh stainless-steel surrounds which were completely at odds with the rest of the building. As if it was wearing an ill-fitting coat it sat unhappily whilst the modern world of finance pulsated within.

Serena stood and regarded her street, wondering again what on earth had ever possessed her to buy the *apartement*. She now referred to such decisions as 'blips'. The imposing front door was covered in dust from the constant traffic. She plunged into the gloom and pulled herself up the wide stone steps. As she passed the *notaire's* door, she paused and stuck her tongue out. She imagined the pale unsmiling woman scratching away at her paperwork with her elderly father blinking nervously beside her. The stone gargoyle above her own door with the electric light bulb spewing out of its mouth stared down at her as she struggled with the lock.

But stepping inside she was hit by the realisation that she was entering a rather beautifully preserved space. The *apartement* was quietly elegant, and its familiarity was strangely comforting. This had been after all her home. She flung back the double doors into the drawing room, and remembered lying on the sofa, the day of her stroke. She stood rooted to the spot as the memories rained down on her.

The fish tank sat empty and was a horrid little reminder of things she would rather not remember. They had all cried when the fish had died. Her mother had said she had never heard such nonsense. 'It's not the fish we're crying for' Serena had said feeling distinctly stupid. 'What is it then?' her mother had demanded. 'Everything' Serena had sighed. 'Everything and nothing'. It had made perfect sense to her as it had to Sebastian and Scarlett, but to explain was beyond them all. It was all the unspoken words, all the pent-up frustration and unfinished business that lingered in the air.

'Anger issues' someone had helpfully suggested. 'Probably,' Serena had agreed thoughtfully and pushed it further down inside her so that the serpent wouldn't rise and show its ugly writhing hissing head. She wandered into her bedroom, the coolness of the smooth tiles urging her to kick off her heavy shoes. The kettle whistled happily and broke her reverie. Loud thumping music drifted up from the streets as slow moving traffic pushed its way through the rush hour. She breathed deeply, inhaling the familiar smells and felt them silently caressing her. She pulled out her favourite mug and felt a pang of remorse that she had neglected to take it back to England with her. Perhaps she hadn't really believed that she would ever really leave France. It held the stains from when it was last used so she methodically wiped it with kitchen cleaner then noticed the thick layer of dust that had settled everywhere since her last visit.

If anyone had asked her to recall the last time she had been here she would struggle to be precise. The final weeks before she heaved herself onto a plane back to her home country were a blur. The fridge contained a half-eaten chocolate bar which still looked edible and a half bottle of wine. Serena pulled it out hesitantly and sniffed its contents, blanching at the acid sharpness that hit her. As she was pouring it away, the front door buzzed. It was her artist friend Moofy, already slightly dishevelled and swaying. 'Hi doll' she drawled in her distinctive deep American accent. They hugged enthusiastically, and stepping back, looked each other up and down approvingly.

'Shit girl' Moofy drawled, 'it's dreary up here, reckon we should go find ourselves a drink'. Serena briefly wondered if it was possibly slightly too early and then dismissed the thought. The culture was different here, perfect for alcoholics really. The ex-pat community spent long afternoons sprawled in various cafés and bars around the central square. The trees would be already be casting their shadows over the tables and Serena was eager to kick off her heavy shoes and catch up with her old friends. She automatically reached down to pick up the empty bottle to take it to recycling. The sound of the large bin downstairs in the street being emptied every morning always made her wince with the crashing of breaking glass. 'Christ you've started already' Moofy said, mistakenly but admiringly.

It was as though Serena had never been away as her feet trod the familiar pavements and she bid a fond 'Bonjour' to the boutique and café owners. She felt rather pale in comparison to the sun-kissed girls they passed, happily flaunting bare toned legs. It wasn't long before they reached the main square where a crowd of her friends were already seated at a table with two carafes of wine on the go. They greeted her as though they had only seen her the previous day and it wasn't long before they all fell into a companionable huddle, laughing as they recalled some of their previous escapades. They had all had their fair share of knocks in life and silently supported each other, packing and unpacking each other's emotional baggage in a gallant fashion as though the very act itself would resolve the problems. Thinking of some of her own baggage, Serena looked about her in a wary fashion. Would she always feel that she needed to be on her guard, and that being divorced from a spook was a penalty for life?

After a while, when far more empty bottles than would be considered acceptable back home littered the table, Serena began to unwind. The prickly feeling she had experienced earlier had dissolved. The group were in the process of organizing an impromptu party that evening and Serena felt light headed from the journey and the afternoon's wine. Serena felt as though she had been transported from one world to another without enough time to adjust; from people laden with fraying rucksacks and whining pasty-faced children at the airport to this gracious square, filling now with locals on their way home from work or dressed to go out for the evening.

Women wore dainty impractical pointed shoes and carried expensive handbags, tossing their hair and laughing throatily. *'Attention, Serena!'* She looked up as her friends playfully threw a napkin at her and lured her back into their conversation which had invariably shifted to sex, and who was sleeping with whom. Celine, an impossibly well coiffured and immaculately manicured yet timid blonde looked perplexed as she considered the subject.

'I think it is all highly overrated' she opined and fumbled in her handbag for a cigarette. She lit up and then exhaled meaningfully 'Unless it's with a much younger man' she added. The others refreshed their glasses and smirked. 'Well when was the last time you had sex anyway?' Moofy asked. Lena, a vibrant Australian well known for her voracious appetite for men scornfully told them they were all 'sexually uptight misguided, frustrated and unadventurous'. The rest of the women bristled with indignation as she laid this conversational gauntlet before them. Their gorgeous gay friends Orlando and Hugh, sensing fun and a heated debate, brightened considerably and ordered another bottle. Serena felt momentarily embarrassed as she became aware their conversation was being listened in on by several people nearby, now quite riveted.

'Tell us about your sex life then, Serena' they chorused loudly. She was ready for them. 'Every which way' she retorted. 'I'm so exhausted by it all I can hardly speak'. 'One of your lovers is over there' Moofy said provocatively if inaccurately. 'At least it's only the one' she parried laughingly. Some-days this crowd would sit and count the numbers as they spied old flames and laugh, although not unkindly, at each other's stupidity and heartache, as various rushed romances turned into farces worthy of a situation.

Orlando turned to Serena 'You're looking well, darling'. He was the more boisterous of the two and was prone to joining them all for nights out when Hugh was away. They would crawl the bars, sometimes falling into the seedy transvestite night club. When such evenings ended there Serena would vow never to return but there was an easy-going camaraderie amongst the queens who flaunted high firm bosoms and impossibly long lean fishnet clad legs. 'There's plenty more room here for extra tarts' they would chorus, 'especially ageing one's' they would add bitchily.

Serena and her friends would sit and chat and scrounge cigarettes and complain that the wine was warm, nasty and overpriced. Sad, lonely looking men, mostly farmers from rural villages lured into town by the promise of anonymous sex propped themselves against the bar and looked hopeful. The female owner (although it was rumoured that she had had a sex change) regarded them all with kindly disdain. She was always surrounded by young, muscular and attentive men. They gigglingly speculated that she must be impossibly tight 'down there' and thus have an unfair advantage over those of them who had given birth. Once Lena had confided that she had had 'an extra tuck down there' and Abbey startled them all by announcing rather bluntly that it was a complete waste of money when trying anal sex could have spared her the expense. This kept them all quiet for a while until the bravest asked 'With whom?' When she admitted his identity, they all spluttered with laughter as it was the solemn looking man from the *boulangerie* who handed Serena her baguette every morning. After these nights they would all roll home hanging onto each other and making an unseemly racket in the deserted cobbled streets.

By this time the group had become sprawling and ungainly as more people attached themselves to the friends, sensing some fun in store. They expressed surprise and delight at Serena's impromptu return. 'I love and miss you all' she slurred and meant it at the time. What was love anyway? Merely an emotion of the moment, an expression of deep fondness bestowed on your nearest and dearest. She was never going to fall in love again anyway. Sitting in the sunny square she felt mollified and tranquil.

Once they had dispersed with promises to meet in a couple of hours she returned home and spent an hour or two discovering items she had forgotten about. Clothing she had scorned and left behind without so much as a backward glance now became a source of comfort to her. An old dressing gown she had nearly tossed aside for good hung on its lonely hanger waiting for her to stroke it and breathe in its familiar scent. They say familiarity breeds contempt, she thought, yet familiarity was breeding a kind of contentment. Serena lay down on her old iron bed and felt glad to be alone for a short while. The crack in the ceiling which had once worried her, now barely registered.

Once she had dozed off and recovered from the journey and the alcohol she padded into her bathroom. It was all so terribly 'French' with its erratic plumbing and gurgling pipes. The large enamel bath was completely impractical, needing copious amounts of hot water to give a decent wallow. She was particularly proud of her handsome vintage spacious sink with its distinctive taps. It was so satisfying to have originals instead of cheap imitations although she knew the latter were so much more practical. The vast iron radiators which gathered dust at an alarming rate had been an extravagant purchase, but after the cold of the Château heat and comfort were hugely important to her and they had been appreciated by her guests.

Serena quite fancied a ride along the nearby Canal du Midi but calculated that she wouldn't have time today. She had loved cycling on its narrow path under the plane trees and feeling the air blow through her hair as she soaked up the open countryside. At this time of year, she remembered, the trees would be just beginning to show their first delicate bright green leaves which gave everywhere an invigorating air though their roots would threaten to dismount you unless you were careful.

The wild flowers growing along the banks were a delight. Deep purple wild irises nestled in the hedges, Queen Anne's Lace flowered in profusion, delicate and gentle, and abandoned fields of vibrant red poppies danced in the breeze. Those rides taken alone with only her camera for company had been a great solace, and she would find herself hurriedly dismounting and flinging her bike carelessly in the lush new grass as she scrambled with her camera to capture her favourite sights.

The tourists churned up the muddy waters as they cruised by in their hire boats although Serena couldn't see the pleasure in going at such a slow pace. When the weather was wet, they would huddle miserably on top of their boats shivering in flimsy waterproofs their eyes set resolutely ahead.

On hot days, wives and girlfriends would sunbathe on the front decks whilst the men steered. At times like these, the shade from the trees was a blessing and only the gentle throbbing of the engines would disturb the summer silence. At night the barges were tethered to banks and their occupants would sit on deck, drinking wine.

These holidaymakers would rub shoulders uneasily with gangs of travellers, hell bent on drinking copious amounts of strong lager. Dogs with glassy, yellow eyes roved around them urinating and fouling the grass whilst they lay stoned, disregarding the distress it caused as they flouted the law. The *gendarmes* mainly ignored them unless one of them became so drunk that it was public nuisance or if they stumbled into the smarter cafés scrounging cigarettes.

Serena had just lowered herself into a decadently full bath when the doorbell buzzed. 'Blast' she muttered under her breath and pulled herself out, dripping water all over the uneven but beautiful floor tiles. These had been hidden under a layer of concrete for many years, but she had lovingly revealed and restored them, finishing her knees off forever. Flinging on her ancient dressing-gown, she went to open the heavy wooden door and looked down at her friends, who were standing a couple of steps below her. These could sabotage the unwary; people had been known to fall down them and she herself had once fallen *up* them, after a particularly memorable evening.

There they stood, freshened up and sporting colourful clothing for the evening ahead. 'I'm in the bath' she said grumpily, but this didn't remotely faze any of them and they pushed past her laughing, bottles at the ready. Soon her kitchen cupboards were being opened as they hunted for glasses and squeezed ice out of plastic trays. Music filled the air as her quiet space was once more filled with life.

'I don't know how fresh the ice cubes are' she warned them. Everyone stopped momentarily in their tracks to consider this. 'Can ice go off?' asked Celine, a frown crossing her normally unreadable features. 'Like anyone cares or gives a shit' Moofy replied dismissively. 'Just pour the frigging drinks' and she held her glass up rudely to Celine's face. 'Hell, take a chill-pill' Celine said crossly as Serena ambled back to the bathroom to resume her *toilette* in lukewarm water.

The sound of them all arguing amused her until they all trooped into the bathroom and surrounded her, dragging in various chairs. Protecting her modesty with a strategically placed flannel and loofah, she nevertheless felt rather nonplussed until Moofy handed her a glass of delicately bubbling champagne. Serena placed this on the wide shelf of the bath. Just then a song which had particularly painful associations cut through the air.

'Jesus, I hate this song' she said passionately at which point Moofy began dancing round the room waving a half empty glass. Orlando looked at her rather crossly and told her 'to get over herself'. Abbey then remarked that Serena had put on weight, so they all looked at her submerged form appraisingly. In the wake of her separation from Randolph, she had lost so much weight that Sebastian and Scarlett had told her that she was skeletal. She chose not to notice her drawn face but rejoiced in her skinny thighs whenever she saw them reflected in shop windows.

Her girlfriends had been envious when she reported that she could now slip into an impossibly tiny bikini which Randolph had bought back from one of his trips abroad. Scouring the duty free for a hasty and guilty present, he must drunkenly have been thinking of a dusky lover's figure rather than Serena's. It had lain in a drawer for years, symbolising the farce that their marriage had become, until one day she had taken it to a hot Mediterranean beach and lain on the soft sand next to a ridiculously impractical man, feeling a defiant thrill shoot through her.

'Yes, I have put some weight back on' she said to Abbey now 'but you're a bitch for mentioning it!'. Sweet, thoughtful and gentle Hugh smilingly patted her bare shoulder and told her she was adorable just the way she was. Serena smiled back mistily, remembering the time when she had lain on the hard-narrow hospital bed feeling helpless and inadequate and longing to be free.

This gang had all trooped in, bearing ridiculous amounts of chocolate, and gossipy magazines and books too heavy for her to lift Moofy had purloined a wheelchair and triumphantly pushed it into Serena's room, where they helped her out of bed and recklessly wheeled her towards the lift. A young French doctor had challenged them mildly but they had flirted with him shamelessly. He waved them away smilingly revealing the most perfect set of teeth, offset by sexy dark stubble on his strong chin.

Lena went into lascivious detail about what she would do if she ever found herself alone with the doctor, as the lift descended to the ground floor. Wheeling Serena outside, they teased her that she was in a mental institution and would never have been released had they not kidnapped her, so when she eventually took large gulps of the sweet summer air she was half-laughingly resigned to her fate. But the sunflowers that were just beginning to bloom in the distance seemed like dots of pure gold.

The song with unfortunate associations came on again, and Serena suspected that they had played it deliberately. But she was becoming immune, floating nicely on the champagne. She didn't care that her skin was crinkling. The doorbell went again, and she heard more people entering the *apartement*. It appeared that she had a party on her hands. Alone now, she got out of the bath, towelled herself dry, and slipped on her tightest white trousers and a sleeveless, burnt orange silk top.

The music was now turned up to an unsociable volume and the new arrivals greeted her enthusiastically. 'How's the UK then Serena'? someone asked. 'So so, you know' she answered automatically, for this was all that was required of her. As she had wanted to be, she was living purely in the moment, but with people who had joked her back into a sense of herself when it had really counted.

Two black people-carriers with tinted windows eventually arrived, and they messily poured themselves inside them. Serena slumped back deep into the leather clad interiors and watched the outside world slide by. From the dreary narrow grey streets of the town they sped into the countryside, where vineyards stretched as far as the eye could see. The villages they passed through were small and appeared deserted. Eventually the cars turned through tall wrought iron gates into a steep gravel driveway. Either side were bushes of neatly rounded lavender with their tiny flower heads just starting to appear. Inside the darkened car the talk turned to the host and hostess who were a wealthy couple of Americans. They had purchased the château and its sprawling vineyard for fun. Moofy was in her element having just taken a call for another portrait commission. 'Last fucking client died on me' she explained 'although the widow was so overcome with gratitude that the portrait was finished, that she used it on his memorial sheet'. She shrugged apologetically, 'Kinda freaky huh'.

'Oh my god' Orlando broke in, 'that's just absolutely awful' and he threw up his hands in mock horror. The château came into sight and for a split second, Serena was piercingly reminded of her beloved former home which she had fought so hard to try and keep. The carved wooden front was freshly oiled to keep the fierce heat and unrelenting winds of the Corbieres from ruining it. The heavy steel door knocker was fashioned into a bunch of grapes. Hugh was uncharacteristically bitchy and remarked that it looked like someone's haemorrhoids hanging out of their backside and they all choked and stifled their laughter.

Celine whose friends their hosts were, turned around and told them all to behave. The door swung open and a tiny, birdlike woman of indeterminate age appeared. She had blonde shoulder length hair and was wearing a richly-hued long silk roble. On her feet were gold strappy sandals from which immaculately painted jet-black toenails peeped out. A chunky gold serpent hung round her neck, tiny green twinkling emeralds for its eyes.

'Hi' she said, the 'i' in the greeting elongated so much that they could all have tripped over it. Serena was regretting not only the afternoon but the early evening indulgence and thought wistfully of her beautifully made bed and Egyptian cotton sheets. She clearly wasn't used to this pace of life any more. They shuffled inside proffering various gifts. Orlando was clutching an extravagantly wrapped assortment of locally handmade chocolates which Moofy had raided in the car, claiming to be peckish. It had been a struggle to repackage them satisfactorily. Hugh who was by far the politest of the bunch remarked pleasantly what charming home the hostess had, and she beamed at him appreciatively.

Serena cast her eye round the house, noticing every detail. She found it to be in poor taste though obviously a lot of money had been spent. Monstrously heavy dark furniture and ornate tapestries filled the cavernous spaces. But she did approve of the many vases of white lilies scenting the air with their fragrance. Their hostess ushered them through corridors until they came to a set of glass doors at the back of the house which opened onto a deep terrace. Dusk was falling, and the last rays of the sun illuminated the horizon. Groups of immaculately dressed people were circulating graciously. Women with long scarlet painted nails clutched glasses of champagne, the diamonds in their ears and round their wrists sparkling and dancing in the light. Serena had forgotten how much everyone dressed up over here and was glad that she had donned her glad rags.

'Oh my god' muttered Abbey under her breath as she took in the scene. 'I hate this sort of do'. Abbey had been a warden in a high security psychiatric hospital in her previous life and had the ability to spot unbalanced person at ten paces. She was also trained in self-defence and was more than capable of throwing a punch if some hapless man overstepped the mark. 'I thought you would feel right at home here darling' Orlando whispered. '

'Surrounded by people who all look in need of therapy, you mean' she scoffed. And there was something unrealistic and false about the whole crowd. A man whose lined features and deep tan made him resemble a pickled walnut swept up to them.

'A very warm welcome dear ladies and gentlemen', he smiled, bowing graciously to them all. His greeting was genuine enough and Serena felt guilty about her critical appraisal, though she couldn't help observing that his teeth and hair were obviously false, and she couldn't mistake the sadness in the faded blue eyes. She guessed he must be in his eighties, and almost old enough to be his wife's father.

'I adore your mustard suede loafers' Serena told him and then immediately regretted her shallow remark. What on earth was the matter with her? She didn't need to curry favour with him. But he responded by smiling charmingly and waved his hand towards tables dotted in-between vast tubs filled with white geraniums. A middle-aged man dressed in a dinner jacket offered them a tray of glasses. Serena later learnt that he was their English butler who travelled all over the world with them. This afforded him a lifestyle way beyond his wildest dreams. The male guests began to inch their way towards Serena's group, eyeing up the women. Lena had already begun to act up. 'A quick fix of Viagra will sort these old darlings out' she announced, not at all discreetly.

'Oh Lord, are you offering, would you really? Celine looked aghast at the very thought. Moofy nudged Serena hard. 'Doll' she hissed, her glass precariously balanced in her hand, 'get a load of those oysters over there'. Serena focused her attention on the glistening molluscs rather than the ageing lotharios and hoped she could get to the table inconspicuously. No-one else appeared to be interested in the food, chatting away with their heads cocked politely to one side.

'Let's go for it' Serena said under her breath. The two of them moved stealthily towards their goal. Once there they helped themselves to wafer thin slices of bread spread with *foie gras* served with small tubs of fig confiture. Other guests soon joined them, and they sat down. Waiting staff appeared with three different kinds of asparagus, and jugs of melted butter. Crushed black pepper and sea salt in pots were by every place, set with silver cutlery and fine old bone china. Serena was tempted to turn her plate over to find the maker's mark but that would have been rude. She guessed it was a Limoges pattern, classic and understated but fetching little in today's auction houses.

A lady of some considerable size wearing glistening pink lipstick settled down next to Serena. 'What do you do, honey?' she said pleasantly enough. 'What do I do indeed. I'm taking some time out at the moment.' she replied, then making an effort, she returned the question. 'And what about you'?

The lady smilingly replied 'My name is Martha and I'm married to Sydney over there' she said, pointing out a distinguished looking man in a tone of voice that showed she regarded this as an achievement. Serena pulled back her shoulders, knocked back her drink and resolved to be nice. She congratulated Martha on her impeccable taste and turned to Sydney who had moved over to join them.

'So what do you do to amuse yourself Sydney'? Serena asked light heartedly. He didn't look like as if he needed to work, but he had a wicked smile and his eyes twinkled in a naughty fashion.

'I'm just an old film producer' he shrugged apologetically. Before Serena could follow up on this, their hostess pulled over another highly tanned man with a head of distinguished grey hair. He looked the women up and down appreciatively.

'Hiya y'all' he said, 'I'm Randy'. 'Finally, some honesty' Lena shrieked 'So am I honey, so am I' and she moved closer to him to stake her claim for the evening. Serena couldn't help herself, she roared with laughter She had forgotten how mischievous her friends were. The night sky was deepening to a pinkish purple. Swallows darted about in the air above their heads. Celine was discreetly taking photographs and was in a world of her own. Martha had clasped Moofy to her bosom on finding out she was a portrait artist of some distinction.

Sydney was next to Serena now and she had time to observe his designer shirt and beautifully pressed trousers. He had an easy continental style which he effortlessly pulled off. 'So, Serena' said Sydney warmly 'What do you do?' Serena was discomfited to be asked this again She couldn't think of anything remotely interesting to say to this astute and talented man. 'Oh dear' she replied, 'Well, my life is really rather bland and unexciting at present' then silently cursed herself for being so wet.

But Moofy, by now flying nicely thanks to the champagne she had sunk leant over and interjected. 'She's written a book' she said proudly pleased that she could champion her friend. Sydney looked very interested, but Serena felt absurdly self-conscious.

'Who hasn't written a book?' she said shrugging apologetically

Martha joined in the conversation.

'Well, I certainly haven't honey, has anyone else?' She looked around at them questioningly. 'No' they all chorused and looked enquiringly at Serena. Flickering candles in sleek shiny glass holders softened lines and blemishes on lived-in faces. The butler reappeared with another bottle and they started to gather round, settling on comfortable cushions. The realisation that they were expecting her to say anything about her book filled her with dismay. She stepped forward head bowed and an unwanted memory it made her wince. She was back at school and about ten years old. Because she was a chatterbox, they had separated her from her twin in the hope that she would work harder. How wrong they were; she had only bothered with English and Art, her two favourite subjects and felt that she was the victim of an inept and insensitive teacher. She had been accused of being lazy when in fact her natural enthusiasm for learning had been crushed.

But what did any of that matter now? Tentatively at first but gaining in confidence as she realised that people were really listening to her, she began to outline her tale. She scarcely recognised her own voice but sensed that her audience were entertained. Or (she thought, forever the cynic) they were so merry that they'd listen to any old rubbish. Drawing to a close, she said 'And − er − that's it'.

Everyone was strangely silent. The Moofy stood up, hugged and high-fived her, and turning to the others demanded 'Now isn't that one hell of a story?'

Serena blushed and looked at her feet. One well-groomed woman who had seemed shocked when Serena described the attic space in which she had slept, asked her cautiously: 'But didn't you mind sleeping in that shitty space'?

'Of course I did' replied Serena. 'But I had no other choice. Either I paid the bills or risked losing my home again. And things were a hell of a lot easier without Randolph constantly sabotaging things' she said, discovering that she could now joke about him. She stretched her neck and rolled her head from side to side, as if to relieve a headache, when she simply felt drained by reliving her memories.

'That sure was one hell of a roller-coaster ride' Sydney commented. 'So what's next for you?' 'God knows' Serena replied 'I paid a heavy price for misplaced loyalty and a couple of wrong decisions and I got nothing in return'.

'In what way did you pay the price'? he asked compassionately. 'Wel I lost everything' she said miserably, shoulders drooping, and wondering if he had really *heard* what she had just recounted. He smiled at her in a way which told her that he had in fact listened to her with great attention

'That just means you had everything you needed to begin with and next time you'll know how to hang onto it. Some people never get tha chance'.

'I don't think I'll get another chance' she said, forlornly. 'I'm not sure I have the strength or the will any more, to begin all over again'. The champagne-high had worn off and she felt deflated and desperately weary.

He looked at her consideringly. 'I think it could make a good film' he said slowly. 'It has all the ingredients that we Americans just love abou our crazy cousins, the Brits.'. Serena considered those ingredients Though Randolph might get some kind of ego-massage from seeing himself portrayed on the big screen, he would undoubtedly try and sue her. She could hardly bear to think about it. Sensing her hesitation Sydney patted her on the shoulder.

'Let's meet up again soon' he suggested, 'when our heads are clearer But by the way, you *do* still have everything.' He pointed towards he heart. 'It's all inside there. Maybe you've just forgotten how to unlock the door'.

'I think I lost the bloody key years ago' a touched but embarrassed Serena muttered.

It was time to go. Making their farewells, the friends clambered back into the people carriers. Serena leant her head on Orlando who in turr was curled up next to Abbey. In the second car, Moofy, Celine and Hugl made a delightful sleepy trio whilst Lena was in a corner with an adoring Randy who was hanging onto her every word.

As they neared the city Serena felt the sense of claustrophobia which always engulfed her as the buildings closed in. The driver apologised a he pulled up at the crossroads several yards from Serena's street. 'Nea as I can get you, I'm afraid' he said. Large plastic dustbins sat on the kerbside overflowing with garbage, their contents spilling out onto the pavements, leaving an unpleasant stench in the warm air.

By the time she had reached her door the car had pulled away out of sight. The early morning city was profoundly silent, save for a sudden scream from the drug addict in the next street. Serena shivered, remembering watching in horror from her kitchen window as the body of one of her neighbours was removed from her house. The rumour was that she had been dead for at least a week. Serena looked on sadly, as men wearing white suits, face masks and protective gloves stripped the house. Underwear, photographs, a *batterie de cuisine* and finally a bed were carelessly flung into a skip; the pitiful remnants of a lonely life.

Fumbling in her handbag, Serena was wishing she hadn't drunk quite so much when she felt a sudden tingling of fright and unease. Alarmed, she found her key and pushed it into the lock. Swinging open the heavy door, she slid into the cold dark interior. At once, she felt pressure on the other side and realised that someone was trying to follow her inside.

'Non' she screamed forcefully and pushed as hard as she could against the ancient wood. Just before the door slammed, she caught a glimpse of a slightly stooping figure. It was all over in seconds, but she knew at once that it was Randolph.

When she woke the next day she briefly wondered if the previous night had all been a surreal dream; the party, the conversation with Sydney and the split second when she had pushed the door against Randolph. But making tea, she felt sure he had been hiding in the shadows of the doorway opposite waiting for an opportunity to harass her. She felt scared and apprehensive. What on earth did he want with her now? Perhaps it hadn't been a good idea to return.

Later that day she was sorting through one of many boxes of paperwork, when she across a familiar padlocked box. She recalled that she had placed all the loose keys in a bag and once she had found that, the tiny key with a yellow ribbon made it easily distinguishable from the others. Not wanting to be disturbed, she checked that the front door was locked before she opened the box. Holding her breath, she lifted the lid. And there was the gun. She removed it from the padded lining and stroked the hard steel weapon with trembling fingers. Not giving herself time to think what she was doing, Serena loaded it and slipped it inside the hidden pocket of her denim jacket. 'Better safe than sorry' she thought to herself but subsequently wondered if she was being melodramatic.

In the following days, she was acutely conscious of its silent presence as she went about her business. She was wary of straying too far from the safety of her home and would scan the street nervously before leaving or entering. Her friends accused her of being turning into a recluse, as she turned down several invitations. Sydney kept him promise and phoned her.

'I haven't forgotten you' he said but couldn't persuade Serena to agree to meet and talk. She made the excuse that she was too tied up with her business but would get back to him. In fact she was being extremely cautious about what she said on the phone, in case it was tapped. She also suspected that her internet activity was being monitored. By whom and why she had no idea, but she checked and self-censored her emails and blog posts anyway. Randolph's paranoia must have filtered down to her over the years.

When a couple of weeks passed without incident Serena ventured out more, pushing the fear of Randolph following her away. She had found a couple who were interested in renting the *apartement* from her and continuing to run it as a *chambre d'hôte*. The overheads were ridiculous and she couldn't think what else to do in the short term. It would fund her return to England and free her from the risk of a confrontation with Randolph. She began the painful business of de-cluttering and packing. Her own possessions weren't a problem, but Randolph had left behind the most extraordinary amount of clutter and refused to collect it.

The clearing process was intensive, laborious and lonely. The previous owner had never emptied the attics, so she was constantly climbing up and down stairs. Having agreed a date for the tenants to move in, her time was limited now. It was terribly hard to turn her back on the home she had created. She shed a few tears as she folded up baby clothes wondering where the years had gone. By a strange irony, though purchased in London, they were impossibly *chic* French rompers and dungarees. Serena had never imagined then that she would live in France and that her bilingual children were assumed to be French.

Unearthing a wooden farm that her father had made for the children she paused briefly. The pond had long since lost its shiny surface and the fuzzy grass had been worn smooth by use. She placed the farmer and his wife side by side by the front door. The black and white collie dog sat contentedly next to the fat brown cat whilst the two young children peered over the stable door at the horses within.

'Happy families' she muttered sarcastically before swiping it all away angrily. 'Welcome to the real fucking world' she shouted as the figures lay scattered on the dusty attic floor. She couldn't take anything much back with her on this trip as she was flying, but she remembered to take her favourite mug this time. It was printed with the saying 'Only boring women have tidy houses'. It had been a present from her mother; odd really, since her mother was the tidiest person she knew. 'Is that really so?' she wondered aloud. Her homes had been so large and impractical she had seemed to be forever cleaning them. What a waste of time and effort.

Orlando phoned and said he was having a birthday party which Serena simply must go to before she flew home. She had pretty much finished sorting things out and allowed herself to be persuaded. Anxious though she was to turn her back on her French life, it was a good opportunity to say goodbye to her friends.

They were kicking off the evening with drinks on Hugh and Orlando's terrace which had stunning views of La Cité, Carcassonne's medieval citadel. She had cycled over to their house, feeling carefree and light hearted. Problems receded when you were pedalling furiously.

The sinking sun was staining the castle walls blood red, in stark contrast to the indigo of the night sky. Celine was taking lots of photographs. 'I can never tire of this beautiful castle of ours' she sighed, and Serena had to admit that it was a stunning sight.

The shadows of people walking around the inner walls of the castle cast ghostly figures on the ancient stone. Serena had explored the citadel's narrow stone alleyways many times both in the early dawn and late evening and knew all its secret places. The tourists who trudged up through the crowded main alleyway and took only a few cursory snaps were missing out on so much of its magic. There was a hidden side to the castle, and in spring, long grasses dotted with poppies grew luxuriantly. It was, Serena thought, as if the victims of the castle's bloody history were commemorated by the vibrant flowers. For every fallen soul – and every year – a seed stirred beneath the rich soil.

At certain times of day, it was possible to walk around the perimeter wall and not see anyone else. Serena had often closed her eyes, taken a breath and let her imagination transport her back in time, her fingers brushing the crumbling stonework. Sometimes she felt she could almost touch the ghosts of those who had died on the slopes beneath the castle as they drifted past her. The buildings in the twisting streets that led up to the citadel would have been insanitary hovels, their occupants riddled with disease and struggling with poverty. These days they were *bijou* holiday lets. There were those who dismissed Viollet-le-Duc's restoration as merely a Disneyland recreation, but he had undoubtedly saved the ancient castle for posterity.

Orlando moved the party on to a terribly fashionable venue in Rue Trivalle. The bar was crowded with people juggling cigarettes and glasses of wine, but he led them into a garden. They all sat down expectantly under an olive tree, nibbling on sun dried tomatoes and sipping glasses of chilled wine. Serena was conscious of relaxing back into her old frame of mind. She had reined in her once crazy lifestyle to a degree, but she wasn't prepared to step down so much that she felt squashed and squeezed as the walls of conformity closed in around her. Nor did she want to think too deeply about any of it tonight; she just wanted to have one last laugh with her friends. Leaning forward, she pressed Lena to 'spill' about her continuing affair with Randy.

When the evening was over, they all kissed each other on both cheeks, promising to keep in touch and wishing Serena *Bon Voyage* and *Au Revoir*. She supposed she had better push her bike rather than risking falling off it, as she had once before. The lights of Le Pont Vieux which linked the old town with the new, bathed the old stone with a yellowish glow. Moths and other night insects were drawn to the lamps. Indistinct animal noises drifted up from the jet-black water below. Serena shuddered as she peered down over the low walls, wondering for a split second what it would be like to lie on the river bed whilst creatures swam gently round her.

Raising her eyes to the skies above Serena observed the scurrying clouds above her and hoped that all her anxieties would disperse as swiftly. She paused at the ancient stone cross which marked the territory between the old and new towns. For centuries there had been tension between the two but now they combined to celebrate the city's history and folklore, if mainly for the benefit of the tourists.

Feeling slightly unsteady on her feet, Serena found the firm handlebars of the bike reassuring. There was a slight uphill slope to the bridge which made moving forwards more of an effort. Looking ahead she saw the sudden flare of a cigarette lighter. Someone was sheltering in one of the parapet's curved recesses.

'Bugger' she cursed softly under her breath, belatedly realising the folly of going home alone. It was probably only an intoxicated traveller, but she must take control and mount her bike. As she swung her leg over the saddle a figure gradually moved out of the shadows. Struggling to plant her feet on her pedals she almost froze, as she recognised Randolph's unmistakeable limp. He was walking straight towards her, though he didn't look up, preoccupied by his nicotine fix.

'Fuck' she exclaimed inadvertently, and his head snapped up. Now he was a few yards in front of her, blocking her way. It really was him; this was no dream, and he wasn't merely a figment of her imagination. His eyes narrowed in recognition, and he curled his lip distastefully.

'Out drinking again, Serena' he sneered, though as he moved closer, she could see the map of red veins on his cheeks which characterise the true alcoholic. His fingertips were deeply stained by the yellow curling cigarette smoke from the roll ups he chain-smoked. Though formerly a tall man, he seemed to have shrunk. She looked him up and down with disdain.

There was an excruciatingly long moment as they regarded each other. Then he lurched forward, and she was in no doubt that he meant to harm her. So quick was she to react to his movement that his face registered complete surprise, his mouth hanging open slackly, as though he was trying to say something. Afterwards, Serena could never remember how she had evaded his outstretched arm, but he just seemed to melt away. One moment he was there and the next he had just disappeared.

For a few anxious seconds Serena scanned the water but saw and heard nothing. There was no struggling body fighting with the tangled slimy weeds. Trembling, she pushed her bike along the path home as fast as she could manage, though her legs were shaking too much to pedal. She kept looking over her shoulder, frightened that he might be pursuing her, but she reached home safely. For once, ignoring the *notaire's* prohibition, she bolted the front door.

The following morning, Serena wondered if she had imagined their encounter, but didn't want to dwell on it. She had a plane to catch and even Randolph couldn't threaten her in Dorset. Before she left, she locked his gun away in its box and threw it down a disused chimney. She hoped it would remain hidden forever. Soon she was tearfully hugging Sebastian in the searing heat of the airport. 'Time to say goodbye again,' she lamented.

Her lovely son had chosen to stay in Carcassonne where he had made a life for himself and had a good group of friends. Serena understood his decision; after all, he had lived in France for most of his life. But she did so *hate* these goodbyes and tortured herself by wondering how different his life would have been had she not concurred with Randolph's decision to move to France. Whenever she expressed this to either of the children, they would remind her that their fluency in two languages would stand them in good stead throughout their lives. They would also insist that they did have some fond memories of Randolph. When they were still tiny, he would arrange impromptu picnics on little-known beaches, making them feel part of some secret world known only to the privileged few. And when all they could afford were cheap camping holidays in a farmer's field, he had to contrived to turn them into thrilling adventures.

Before he sank into apathy and despair, they had frequently found him hysterically funny. And although they later came to despise the way that he wasted his own intellectual gifts, he had taken an interest in their young minds, encouraging them to read widely and well. They had also enjoyed his effortlessly inventive cooking, and ability to turn a simple supper into a feast. Though Serena was grateful for these comments she couldn't help suspecting that they were triggered by a loving desire to reassure her.

Several weeks passed, and Serena's arrangement with the couple renting the *apartement* seemed to be going well. Money was still tight, but she was earning just enough to sustain her new life in Dorset and enjoying spending more time with her parents.

But then a bombshell – in the form of a registered letter – arrived. It was from the managing agents of her *apartement* and sent on the instigation of her neighbour, the frosty *notaire*. It informed her that unless she closed the business was closed immediately, she would be taking Serena to court for breaching the rules and endangering the peaceful habitation of the house.

Though dismayed, Serena wasn't surprised. She had received a similar threat some years previously, shortly after she'd kicked Randolph out. Calculating that the woman would think she was now more vulnerable, she had confronted the agents and asked them to explain the difference between her business and that of her neighbour's. Generally, she said, her guests stayed for a week or less, silently climbing the stairs to their rooms. In contrast, the *notaire's* many clients were constantly coming in and out of the building unchallenged, because of her insistence that the communal door be unlocked.

'And some of them are criminals' Serena had stated firmly. The agents looked uneasy but told her to ignore the *notaire* and carry on with her business. She had double checked with a second lawyer too, just to be sure. 'Ignore her,' he had advised. He had found just one sentence in the occupancy rules of the building which had been drawn up forty years previously.

'This simply does not apply any more' he had said, 'if it did, half the bed and breakfasts in Carcassonne would be closed down'.

'Does this wording apply to the French as well'? Serena had asked. He had answered with a very Gallic shrug.

Furiously, Serena contacted the agents and reiterated the advice she had previously been given. They revealed that the *notaire* herself had written the occupancy terms all those years ago and in Serena's absence, was now renewing her objections to the use of the *apartement* as a bed and breakfast. Despite Serena's argument that it was the notaire's clients who posed harm to the peaceful and safe habitation of the building, she soon realised that she wasn't going to fend the woman off this time. You simply couldn't take on a French lawyer and win, as Randolph had found out at immense cost. She had no option but to give her tenants notice and close the business. She was effectively forced to sell.

The timing of the ultimatum couldn't have been worse. The French property market had taken a huge nose dive. English people were no longer keen to invest in properties that were plummeting in value. And those who had already been burnt were scrambling to get out, even if they made a loss. Charming châteaux, farms and gîtes no longer lured the English over in droves. The property boom was well and truly over. The French had certainly had their pound of flesh from those English who had been gullible enough to buy into the Peter Mayle dream.

Although it stuck in her craw, Serena instructed her cousin to approach the *notaire* directly. She now owned every other *apartement* in the building except Serena's and it was obvious that she would put obstacles in the way of any sale to a third party. Even so, she drove a very hard bargain.

When Serena returned to Carcassonne to pack everything up, she determined to take the view that possessions were merely objects that are desirable at one point in your life. Yet as the *notaire* pointedly stickered things which she wanted to include in the sale price, she did feel emotionally and practically cheated. When she finally received a cheque for the proceeds of the sale, it was approximately the amount that she realised from the sale of her cottage some fifteen years previously. The irony of this was not lost on her. In every sense she felt she was back where she had started, and a little voice in her head whispered that she should never have allowed herself to be swept along by Randolph's fantasies. She had never really questioned what she herself wanted and needed and as she landed back in England, she resolved that in future she would listen to her instincts.

An Unexpected Death

When Serena saw the announcement on her home page, for a few moments she couldn't take it in.

'R.I.P Randolph' proclaimed the headline, accompanied by a photograph of him grinning whilst holding aloft a full glass of wine.

'Refreshed as usual' was her immediate thought, then as the R.I.P registered, surely this is a joke, albeit a tasteless one? She peered at the picture alongside the stark words. There had to be some mistake; she couldn't be learning of her ex-husband's sudden death on Facebook, of all places? Randolph had continually and derisively dismissed the entire concept of social media as banal. But there it was, instead of − as he would have wished − a solemn obituary in *The Daily Telegraph,* accompanied by a distinguished portrait of him chosen especially for the grave occasion.

Shocked but still disbelieving, Serena wondered whether it could be one of Randolph's own sick pranks. But as she stared at her screen, comments began to appear underneath the post, offering apparently genuine condolences.

'A unique character'

'Will be sorely missed'

'Marvellously witty'

So it must be true...

Picking up the phone she dialled a couple who were mutual friends. The husband was too upset to speak to her and transferred her to his wife who began to sob and haltingly confirmed that Randolph was indeed dead.

'How and when'? asked Serena quietly, needing to know these basic facts.

'Shot in the head' her friend whispered hoarsely, 'There one moment, gone the next'.

'I can't speak any more' she continued softly, 'I know it's early, but I need a drink. I'm so sorry Serena, there were some happy times I know'

She was obviously shocked, but Serena found that she herself wasn't. It was exactly what he had once threatened to do. The reality of the news began to sink in. She looked at her watch. It was 10am on a Sunday morning. *Was* it too early for a drink?

'Randolph's dead' she called up to her new husband Ralph.

Hearing her voice but not the import of her words, he appeared from the top of their narrow stairs nearly hitting his head on the low beam as he descended. 'Impractical house' he muttered and seeing her expression was one of total incomprehension he added 'For tall men' as an explanation.

'Randolph was tall' she replied, adjusting to the past tense. He looked bewildered.

'Disappointment, dismay followed by destruction. I have just summed up Randolph's life' she announced to him. 'And now he's dead.

The words disturbed her with their finality even as she spoke. If he really were dead of course. After their final encounter on the old bridge in France and his subsequent disappearance she had her doubts. A friend would later describe his death as 'an elegant solution'. She poured herself a drink and as the alcohol started to take effect the thought that he could no longer harm her or her children with his vile lies and bitterness lifted her heart slightly.

Was that so terribly wrong after everything that had happened?

Yet when her divorce had come through many of Serena's friends had asked:
'What on earth did you see in him?'
Those who had earned Randolph's respect didn't need to ask this question. Before he began to seek solace in the bottle, he was a natural charmer, who combined a keen intelligence with wit and a great sense of humour.

Serena raised a glass to his memory.

A New Beginning

Serena stopped typing for a moment, and out of her window. She loved the view of the mellow stone church across the road, just visible above the pot of hyacinths she had placed on the sill. She stood, and bending down, breathed in their pleasingly heady scent. There was always something going on outside. People would scurry past on their way to post letters in the red pillar box, sometimes pausing thoughtfully, as if they were weighing up the wisdom of sending a letter or card.

In the novel she was just finishing, Serena had described some beautiful and ancient buildings. Now she lived in another agreeably old house, which wrapped her in its cosy embrace. It was the home she had been searching for all her adult life; a refuge from the storms and dramas of the past. She had been able to rest and reflect. There had been great sadness and great joy in the two years since she had closed the door on the French chapters of her life.

Her wonderful father, her rock, and the source of so much love and support over the years had passed away after a long illness, but though she still grieved for his loss, she was deeply thankful that she had been around to help nurse him. Dignified, loving and supportive to the end, he had teased her about her writing. 'You'll never finish that novel' he had said. Now she felt him urging her on to complete it. She would always be grateful that he had lived long enough to know that she was happily married to Ralph although he had laughingly refused to give her away. 'I've already done it twice and I'm not prepared to jinx this union' he said. So Serena had walked up the aisle on her son's arm.

Hugging herself with glee, she now looked again at the email from Sebastian announcing that he returning to England very soon. As Scarlett already lived locally, Serena would be able to see her beloved children as often as she wanted. For so long, it had been the dearest wish of her heart.

Closing the computer, she reflected that the drama and heartache were over. There were no more chapters to write, and she felt gloriously freed from the past.

Finding Sydney's number, she dialled. He answered almost immediately.

'Randolph's dead' she told him.

THE END

For translation rights and permission queries
please contact the author's agent

Lisa.eveleigh@richfordbecklow.co.uk

Printed in Great Britain
by Amazon